WILDER BROTHERS
RODEO COLLECTION

KALI HART

Wilder Brothers Rodeo Collection is a work of fiction. Names, characters, businesses, places, events, and incidents are either the products of the author's imagination or used in a fictitious manner. Any resemblance to actual persons, living or dead, or actual events is purely coincidental.

Copyright © 2020 by Kali Hart

ALL RIGHTS RESERVED. This book contains material protected under International and Federal Copyright Laws and Treaties. Any unauthorized reprint or use of this material is prohibited. No part of this book may be reproduced or transmitted in any form or by any electronic or mechanical means, including photocopying, recording, or by any information storage and retrieval systems, without express written permission from the author/publisher, except for the use of brief quotations in a book review.

COLT

WILDER BROTHERS RODEO BOOK 1

1

SONYA

"I'm not trying to get arrested," I warn my bestie, Jillian. I've had the *worst* day, but that doesn't mean I'm trying to top any of the events by going to jail.

"We're not going to get arrested, Sonya." With a dramatic roll of her eyes, she tugs my arm, refusing to give up until my feet shuffle forward toward the tear in the fence. "Kicked out maybe."

"This is such a terrible idea."

"It's a great idea!"

"We don't have tickets, and we're not romance writers," I point out, certain my logic will win the ridiculous debate.

"Hence the *hole* in the fence."

Jillian really is the best, even when she's being a tad...rash. She's always had my back, and I know that's what she's trying to do now.

I got a flat tire on the way to work, spilled coffee on my new dress, and was laid off—all in the course of the first two hours of my day. But sneaking into a private pre-rodeo event isn't going to make anything better. Especially if we get caught.

"Why can't we be normal people and get pedicures and binge-eat rocky road ice cream on bad days? Breaking and entering—"

"The fence is already broken."

"We're not even dressed for this." It's my last argument, and Jillian seems to know it.

She winks at me. "You don't need a cowgirl hat or boots to be a romance writer going to a rodeo event." Before I can object—not that I have anything left in my arsenal of objections—Jillian yanks me through the gap in the fence. It's a wonder no one has fixed that, because any number of people might sneak in later tonight during the main event.

"You have to act like you belong here, Sonya. Otherwise they'll know."

"No pressure," I mutter.

We head for the covered stands, blending in with the mob of women—and a couple of guys—headed to a restricted area. I'm not a rule breaker, and this makes me feel incredibly guilty. Like I need to stop right now and crank out a romance novel so I actually belong here.

"What's my name?" I ask Jillian.

"What?"

"My author name. Don't we need those if someone asks?" The last thing I want anyone here to know is my real name, so my bestie better hurry up and create some new identities for us or I'm running for that fence.

Jillian squints her eyes at me, like she's trying to see me in a different light. "Pamela Love."

"That sounds like a porn name."

"Fine. Jane Harper. That sounds romancy enough, right?"

"It's better," I admit, still completely against this scheme. I just know they're going to figure out we don't belong here. We're the only ones without lanyards or cowboy hats.

"I'll be Mandi Flowers." She tugs me along in line, because my feet have apparently stopped working. But I'm not done with my questions. I tend to overthink things—to a fault—and it's happening right now. "What *kind* of romance do we write?"

"Seriously?"

"There's all kinds—contemporary, historical, paranormal, erotica, not to mention the heat levels—"

"You, my dear, are a contemporary western romance author. The steamier the better."

"And you?"

I can tell Jillian is annoyed, but she marches on. True friend right there. "I write vampire shifter romance. There, happy?"

I almost tell her how I don't think her name goes with the genre, but then I see him. Any words I had rolling on the tip of my tongue evaporate. Because the man in the cowboy hat, leaning casually against the fence in front of the stands, is gorgeous. Like movie star meets Greek god gorgeous.

Suddenly, I'm not so nervous about this little scheme.

Jillian nudges me. "You might want to pick your jaw up off the ground."

"Can we have everyone take a seat in the stands, please?" One of the crowd controllers—designated by a blue vest—announces. My common sense is operating on a much lower level than it was minutes ago. I can't peel my eyes away from those Wranglers. The way they hug his hips has me quite hot and bothered.

He's talking to an older gentleman next to him, completely uninterested in the crowd forming in the stands. I quickly scan the dozens of people around me. I can't believe how many writers turned out for this convention.

"Isn't this exciting?" Jillian quietly squeals into my ear. I follow her eye trail to another cowboy off to the side. He's handsome too, but not in the same way as *my* cowboy. "I call that one."

"He's all yours." Because as crazy as this whole let's-make-Sonya-feel-better scheme is, I'm suddenly a big rodeo fan. I try to be discreet and keep myself from staring, but I can't seem to help myself. If I really wrote western romance novels, this rodeo cowboy would be the leading man.

Maybe this day is redeemable after all.

COLT

I'm still not sure how I got roped into this.

Well, I do know. I made a bet with my brother when I knew better.

This whole entertain-the-romance-writers is more Hudson's thing than mine. He loves the attention from the crowd—and the ladies. But me? I just want to focus on my job. I'm here to ride bulls and take home the winnings. Not to entertain a bunch of swoony romance writers in some private behind-the scenes look at the rodeo. Yet, here I am.

"A bet's a bet," says my Uncle Raine, nudging me with his elbow. He cackles at Hudson's wave toward us. It's a good thing that Hudson is a bronc rider.

Because I would make it my personal mission to beat him tonight, just to prove a point. I'm still planning to rack up more points.

"Please, writers. Take your seats. Our cowboys are on a tight schedule." The woman in the blue vest introduced herself earlier, but I can't for the life of me remember her name. I'm horrible with that sort of thing, but to be fair, I meet a *lot* of people. When you're one of the best—which I've worked really hard to be—tons of people want to meet you.

I scan the crowd, not surprised to see at least thirty women. Some are taking pictures. Others are scribbling notes. Most are talking and giggling. I've never read one of those sappy romance novels, but judging from their giddy expressions, they're all convinced this is the perfect setting.

"Remind me why I took that bet again," I say to Uncle Raine. Hudson always beats me at calf roping. I'm better on a bull—not one of my brothers would argue that—but Hudson's always been better on a horse. And with a rope. But he had me riled up the other night, and well, here I am.

"Ladies," says the woman in the blue vest, "and *gentlemen*." She nods to the two men sitting off to the side. I wonder if they might write westerns instead of actual romance. But who am I to judge? It amazes me that anyone could write an entire book, much less make a career out of it. I admire their abilities. I just don't particularly appreciate being their spectacle. "Let's go ahead and get started."

I adjust my stance, forcing myself to push off the fence and flash a smile at the crowd as she introduces me.

"This is Colt Wilder. He's currently ranked third—in the entire world!" The small crowd erupts, but their cheering fades to a dull roar when I see her. She's tucked into the crowd, about halfway up. I try my best to wave to the crowd, pretend I'm not affected by the beautiful brunette, but my eyes keep traveling back to her. *Oh man*. Those green eyes of hers are just...dazzling.

"Welcome, everyone." I give the spiel I've memorized for previous events. Even an anti-social guy like me can't avoid the occasional interview, and I'm thankful for that right now. Because I'm not just nervous, I'm incredibly distracted. Her eyes are locked on me, taking in every word. I swallow hard, eyes suddenly dry cause I can't seem to blink. Why isn't she taking notes like everyone else? At least then she'd have to look at her notepad.

"I'm the oldest Wilder brother—the only bull rider," I continue. "That's my brother Hudson over there, trying to hide."

The crowd laughs, the brunette flashes a dazzling smile, and I finally relax. With that beautiful woman hanging on my every word, I launch into all things rodeo life. I may not be excited about this assignment, but I don't half ass anything.

Besides, the longer I talk, the longer I get to keep the sexy brunette in my sightline. Her smile could brighten the stormiest day. I crave her presence like a man craves a drop of water in a desert, and I've got a plan to spend a little alone time with her soon.

2

SONYA

"Ask him for a picture." Jillian shoves me forward and I nearly stumble right into the cowboy's arms. From the stands I could tell he was tall. But standing inches away from him, my nose almost colliding with his bulging chest muscles, I feel tiny.

"Careful there." He reaches out a hand, steadying me by the elbow. His touch sends a surge of heat through my entire body.

"Can she get a picture?" I hear Jillian call above the crowd. Her little stunt has pushed me to the front of the line now that the behind the scenes session is officially over, and I know there are several narrowed glares piercing my back. I don't dare look.

"Of course." Colt—damn that's such a sexy name

for a cowboy—lifts his arm and cradles me against his side. It feels...perfect.

"You're a romance writer?" he asks me.

Meeting those cobalt blue eyes has me tingly in naughty places. My heart races at the penetrating gaze that I swear can see clear into my soul.

"She sure is," I hear Jillian chime in because words of any kind obviously failed me. "That's Jane Harper you're hugging. Western romance author, the steamier the better."

"Jane Harper." The made-up pen name sounds so delicious escaping those lips that it's easy to imagine I really *am* her. Jane didn't get laid off from her job or splashed by a mud puddle when she tried to assess her flat tire. Jane can be anyone she wants.

"Smile for the camera now." Jillian gives us a little wave and proceeds to snap dozens of pictures, if the scowls of the surrounding women are any indication.

"Thank you," I say to Colt, relieved that the words found their way out of my mouth without tripping. Then again, I'm Jane Harper right now. Jane isn't intimidated by a sexy cowboy. Jane would—

Colt leans down and says in a low voice against my ear, "Can you stick around?"

"Uh—" Sonya Williams would be running before she got popped for breaking into a private event under false pretenses. But Jane Harper is much bolder. "Yes. Yes I can."

"Good. Let me finish up the pictures." His hand lingers on my shoulder, sliding slowly away as another eager writer tries to wedge her way in for a picture. A fiery trail blazes my skin where his fingers grazed. With an intense look that has my heart pounding, he adds, "Hope your day is free."

Heat rushes up my neck and fills my cheeks as I turn away. Jillian yanks me by the arm, away from the mob of fangirling writers—and fanboying. Let's be fair.

"What was *that* about?"

"I—I don't know." My gaze keeps slipping back to Colt, a tinge of jealousy shooting through me as he puts his arms around two women. It's completely irrational. He's basically a celebrity in the rodeo world—a fact I can confirm after everything he told us. Celebrities have fans.

"Well, whatever it is, he's into you."

My eyes lock with Colt's, forcing me to swallow hard. "He wants me to stick around."

Jillian lets out a squeal that turns a dozen heads. I elbow her in the side. "Not so *loud*."

"We're staying, right?"

"Yes."

"That's my girl."

"*That* is Jane Harper."

Jillian squeezes my arm in her uncontrollable

excitement. "And you wanted to binge eat ice cream instead."

"Excuse me, ladies." It's the woman in the blue vest, and her eyes are bouncing all over the two of us. "Where are your lanyards?" Her voice is more nasally with her two feet away from us. "The rules state to wear them the *whole* weekend."

My heart skyrockets in my chest, and I'm certain I'm about to turn fifty-nine different shades of red and blow our cover. The non-rule breaker in me is on the brink of a full-on panic attack.

"We left them at the hotel by mistake," says Jillian, cool as a damn cucumber. I'm not even entirely sure what that phrase means, but she certainly seems to be pulling it off. "We'll make sure we keep them on from here on out, won't we Jane?"

"Yes."

"I don't remember any Jane on our—"

"Ladies." Colt's deep, sexy voice interrupts the conversation. Had I not been so panicked about being caught, maybe I would've sensed his approach. I certainly feel his presence now, wrapped around me like a warm blanket. Or maybe it's my overactive imagination.

"Colt," says the woman in the blue vest, "thank you so much for your time today." She rambles on for a few more minutes, and I send him an apologetic shrug. Like her inability to shut the hell up is somehow my fault. He winks at me, and Jillian squeezes the back of my arm hard enough to cause pain.

"Ladies, it's time to leave," says the woman in the blue vest—Darla her name tag dangling from her lanyard says. "We can't bother this rodeo star any longer. He has a job to prepare for. Come along now."

"Actually," says Colt, "they're my guests for the remainder of the afternoon."

COLT

Darla lifts her clipboard and starts flipping pages. "I wasn't aware—"

"It's a special arrangement." I've been waiting too impatiently to get some alone time with *Jane Harper*. I have a suspicion that's not her real name, but I'm okay with that. Most of these women here have a fake name.

I put my arm around the blue-vested woman who is quickly becoming flustered. From my brief interaction with her earlier, I figured out she doesn't care to be far away from her schedule and lists. I try to usher Darla away, but she fights me and pushes against my arm until she's free to spin around on Jane and her friend.

"What did you say your names were again?" Darla asks.

Something fizzles in the air at that question. Some warning bell or some such thing. Darla is much too organized to have missed anyone on her tidy list.

"Jane Harper and Mandi Flowers," the friend answers.

Darla flips through her clipboard. Maybe I should wait and see what she finds—or doesn't find. But I'm about out of patience. I need Jane all to myself. After I get Darla on her way, I still have to figure out what could occupy her friend.

"Darla, I don't have much time. I appreciate everything you did today. But these ladies are coming with me now."

"But—"

I use a little more force with the arm that ushers her away toward the mob of writers waiting for her at the main gate. "Thank you, Darla. This behind the scenes event went off without a hitch."

"I don't know—"

"I'll see you all tonight." I click the gate to the stands closed, effectively locking it from the inside. This gives Darla no choice but to stand there and yell or go back to the group of waiting writers.

My heart thrums in my chest with each step closer to Jane Harper I get. Something is off, if the blush that colors her cheeks and that beautiful neck is any indication. But I can't find it in myself to care. My eyes are too busy feasting on the curvy beauty in jeans and a soft blue sleeveless blouse. Add a pair of cowgirl boots, and I'd be a goner.

"Sorry about her," the friend says about Darla. "She's been a bit frazzled ever since we arrived."

My gaze lingers on Jane, my eyes dropping to her chest. I swear it was to spot the missing lanyard. But that doesn't stop my imagination from running wild. Her tits are voluptuous. What I wouldn't give to get her in a pair of cowgirl boots—and nothing else.

"It's no bother," I finally say so both women don't think I'm a complete creep for staring too long. But the devious twinkle dancing in both of their eyes tells me I shouldn't be concerned about that.

"You wanted me to stick around?" Jane asks as she bites her bottom lip.

My gaze flickers to her friend, wishing I had a good reason to get Jane all alone. But I get it. I'm a complete stranger. I'll have to earn trust from both of them. "You said you write western romance," I say to Jane, because it sounds like a good excuse for what I'm about to offer.

"Yes, that's right."

"How would you like a private tour?"

"She'd love that," the friend pipes up. "It'll help her with her next book, won't it?" She nudges Jane with her elbow.

"Um, yes. Yes it will."

I extend my arms to both ladies, wishing it were only Jane. "Shall we get started?"

"You know, I actually need to run back to the hotel," says the friend. "But you two knock yourselves out."

"Jill—Mandi!"

I quirk an eyebrow at that, but if they're writers they may not want their real names revealed. Especially with the stranger they *just* met. Also could be some weird rule Darla created for the convention. Maybe the writers aren't allowed to *go* by real names this weekend.

"I write vampire romance." Her friend frees herself from Jane's hold. "Bears and werewolves and stuff. Not a cowboy in sight. This tour won't really do me a lot of good."

"But—"

"I'll come back for the rodeo. Save me a seat?"

"I'll get you both tickets for the VIP section," I offer. "Both nights."

"Both?" Jane repeats, her eyes widening.

"Rodeos are usually two-night events. Surely Darla mentioned that?"

"She did," Mandi says, "remember, Jane?"

"Yes, I think I forgot. Too tied up in the next book and all." Her eyes dance everywhere around me, but they avoid meeting my own. Something is off. Maybe I should call it quits while I'm still ahead. I don't pursue women. I'm not Mr. Womanizer like my brother, Hudson.

How could this ever work between Jane and me? My life is the rodeo. I'm on the road a lot—more than I'm home sometimes. I don't even know where she's from. *But writers can travel*, a voice whispers in my head.

"Ready to start the tour?" I ask before I can talk myself out of it.

"I'll see you two later," Mandi scurries away toward the gate I just locked.

Jane tilts her head up, her dazzling green eyes meeting my gaze. "Lead the way."

3

SONYA

I try my best not to panic when I see Jillian disappear. She's too far away now to call back, and I'm all alone with a cowboy I *just* met. Alarm bells should be ringing obnoxiously in my head, warning me to chase after my bestie before she leaves with the only working vehicle between the two of us. But instead, I feel...*safe*.

"What's your book about?" Colt asks me, extending his arm for me to loop my own through. I hope he can't tell how shaky my entire body is when I do.

"A rodeo cowboy." Thinking on the fly is *not* my forte. If Jillian's scheme hadn't landed me this private tour with a cowboy who is panty-melting hot, I would really hate her right now. But he's definitely the distraction I need to turn this day around.

"Sounds...interesting."

He leads me away from the stands, opening a gate. I follow him to the area behind the VIP seating on the opposite side of the arena.

I don't dare meet that smoldering, assessing gaze. Not when I'm positive my guilty expression tells all. "He wants to be the best in the world. Doesn't have time for love," I continue. I'm shooting from the hip, but so far it all sounds good. I may not be much of a writer outside of dabbling in some short stories in college, but I *do* read.

"Sounds like a guy I know," I hear him mumble under his breath. I'm not sure what it means, considering he seems pretty interested in me. But interest and love are definitely two different things.

"He meets her by chance, or so he thinks."

"Fate?" Colt suggests.

"You know it."

We're behind the stands now, in the area off limits to fans. There are cowboys everywhere, pens with bulls and some with horses, and tents with food. Off in the distance I see several RVs. I wonder if Colt has one of those or if he's staying in the same hotel I'm supposed to be staying in.

I really should feel guilty about this facade. But at the end of the weekend, he'll be gone. I'll be stuck in this town forced to figure out my life. The last thing I want to think about tonight is updating my resume.

"Let me show you around," he says. For the next hour, I listen with piqued interest as he leads me from one place to another. I meet his three brothers and his uncle. They all seem quite surprised to see him showing me around.

I know what I should be doing; asking questions, doing research for my "next book", but the first question is stiff. The second completely obvious. I'm about to give up, but something happens with the third question. I feel the red fade from my cheeks. I'm listening, absorbing every word. Colt's life intrigues me. It sounds like a fantasy. No desk job. No worries about layoffs. Though when he tells me he broke a collarbone a few years back, I cringe. There's certainly more risk in what he does than any desk job would offer.

"That's about it," he says, stopping at the edge of the private parking lot filled with RVs.

"Do you have one of these?"

"Nah. My uncle Raine does. But the rest of us travel together in a truck or two. We hate flying."

Somewhere during our tour, I went from looping my arm in his to holding his hand. I don't even recall when it happened. Being around Colt feels…natural. Like it's always been. When his gaze lands on me, I shiver. I can't keep my eyes from his lips.

"This one here belongs to my Uncle Raine.

Sometimes Aunt Sally travels with him. But this weekend she stayed home." He squeezes my hand. "You want to see inside?"

I should say no. I definitely should say *no*. But Jane Harper doesn't want to play by the rules. "Yes."

COLT

On our quick tour earlier, I ran into Uncle Raine and all my brothers. One of the food tents has a pile of ribs as tall as a mountain, so we should be safe. I shouldn't invite Jane inside the empty RV—I know I won't be able to keep my hands to myself—but I do anyway.

I follow her up the few steps, admiring her curvy ass in those jeans. Yeah, this is *definitely* a bad idea.

"I have to draw for my bull in half an hour," I tell her, mostly to keep talking. If I stop, I don't know what will happen. But it's likely her lipstick will get smeared, and that's about the calmest possibility.

"Is there a certain bull you want to get?" she asks, taking leisurely steps toward the living area. Uncle Raine loves his RV, and he's upgraded everything in here to include the extra cushy couch cushions.

"Hurricane would be my preference." We're stopped in the middle of the living area, standing between two couches. The safest thing to do would be to sit on opposite ones. Instead, I take a step closer, eliminating most of the distance left between us.

"That sounds like a dangerous bull with a name like Hurricane."

A curl of hair dangles along her cheek, and I'd be a fool to pass up the opportunity to tuck it behind her ear. She bites down on her bottom lip as my fingers graze her cheek, which only makes my heart pound faster.

"I bet there's not a scene inside an RV in your novel." I hope she can't hear the shakiness in my voice. Jane—or whatever her real name is—makes me feel things I've never felt before.

"Nothing quite like this," she says scanning the RV. I wonder if it's her way of gathering ideas. Will *this* be in a future book someday?

I've spent my whole life focusing on my career, focusing on being the best bull rider in the world, that I never left time for love. The word shocks me, and I stumble a step backward. It's not possible to be in *love* with her. Not yet.

"How many books have you published?"

"None yet. Still...rewriting."

I'm surprised by this, but I don't read too far into it.

"I'm in need of some inspiration."

Any man with a heartbeat would recognize the

invitation, and he'd be a fool to turn it down. There's something so magnetic not just about Jane, but about the pull between us. I don't think I could leave this RV right now if I tried.

Reaching for her cheek, I tilt her chin up. Our gazes lock together. I give her one solitary moment to tell me to stop. Because once I descend on those lips, it'll be impossible.

"Kiss me," Jane says.

Longing has been swirling between us since the moment I spotted her in the stands, and every pent-up desire flows into the passionate kiss. It's hungry, sensual, possessive. My body ignites with feelings I've never experienced. I know hardly anything about this woman, except that she's supposed to be in my life.

I have to have her.

"Wow," she pants in a breathless whisper when our lips break apart. Her tits are heaving and my dick is half hard. The sight of her swollen lips about does me in.

"Wow is right." Her chest is pressed against mine, and my eyes can't seem to help themselves as they travel south right down the opening in her sleeveless blouse. I get a peak of a blue lace bra.

"How much time do we have?" she asks.

"Not long." I take a step back so there's enough room for my fingers to work the top button on her blouse. "But long enough to give you a little inspiration." A soft moan escapes as I undo a second button. It's enough for me to slip a hand inside and cup her tit. I wish there was time to lose the bra. "Aren't these a thing of beauty."

"You like them?" She's biting that lip again.

I dig my fingers into the top of her bra, exposing her hard nipple. My dick twitches in my jeans, growing harder by the second. We'll have to stop soon or I'll have to face the ridicule of drawing a bull with a hard on. But I can't resist taking that precious nipple into my mouth and suckling it. Her soft, sensual moans alone are worth the risk.

I give the other tit the same attention, wishing we had time to take this further.

"Where are you staying?" I ask.

"Ho—hotel," she pants.

"Good." Reluctantly I cover her nipples with her bra and fix the buttons on her blouse. Her eyes are drenched with desire, and it's nearly impossible to stop things where they are now. "Tonight, I want to finish what we started."

4

SONYA

"Your lips are swollen," Jillian accuses two seconds after we find our VIP seats.

Playing dumb won't do anything but stall the inevitable, but I try anyway. "Are they?"

"Just what kind of *tour* did you get?"

Hiding my guilty smile is impossible, so I don't even attempt it. "It was just a little innocent make out session." But of course, that's not the truth. Innocent and a hot-as-sin cowboy suckling on my nipples don't really belong in the same sentence.

"Is that *all*?"

I hope not. But I don't say so out loud. Jillian and I have been friends a long time, and she knows I'm not the type to sleep with a man I just met. Much less a man who will be leaving town when the weekend is over. But dammit I can't stop thinking about it. I want to know what it would feel like to have Colt buried deep inside me. I'm crossing my legs so tightly right now it's a wonder I don't cut off circulation.

"Sonya!"

"Jane," I correct her. "It's still Jane. *Remember*?" Besides the fact that several of the romance writers from earlier—including their leader Darla—are seated at the opposite end of the VIP stand, I've grown a fondness for my alter-ego. Jane Harper isn't afraid of anything. The idea of trying to write a romance novel has even bounced around in my mind today.

"Okay, *Jane*. What aren't you telling me?"

"He wants to finish what we started," I blurt. Trying to keep anything from my best friend is a lost cause. I tell Jillian everything, and if I don't, she finds a way to get the truth out of me sooner or later. It's easier to have it all out in the open. Besides, I was *bursting* to tell someone.

"Does he know your secret?"

"No." I thought about telling Colt the truth when we were hiding out in the RV, but I couldn't get the words to form. Pretending to be a confident romance writer who's got it all together is way easier than admitting I'm some pitiful girl who got laid off from a job she didn't even really like that much. Considering I'll never see him again when the rodeo leaves town, I wanted him to remember the better version.

"Well, we know what he wants. What do *you* want?"

I bite down on my bottom lip so hard it almost bleeds. "I want to, too."

Jillian squeals as she claps her hands together. "I'm so proud of you right now!" She suffocates me in a side hug.

"You are?"

"Yes! Jane Harper looks good on you, my dear."

The announcer gets the crowd suddenly roaring at the start of the show, and it's impossible to hold any semblance of a conversation now. Instead, we enjoy the show. One cowboy after another—first the bronc riders, then the bull riders.

When it's finally Colt's turn, my heart hammers in my chest. I'm thrilled to see him do what he does best and also nervous he'll get hurt. A broken collarbone was not the only injury he's ever suffered in his career. I try to imagine worrying about him weekend after weekend, year after year. I know he's older than me, but I don't know how old a bull rider has to be to retire.

What would that life be like?

Jillian lets me squeeze her hand when the clock

starts. Colt rocks with the bull, countering each buck with a movement that keeps him on the beast until the buzzer sounds. He hops off and runs toward the fence.

The crowd—Jillian and me included—go wild with cheering.

"You better congratulate that cowboy properly tonight," Jillian says to me.

Tingles dance between my thighs, imaging doing just that. "I plan on it."

COLT

"Do you trust me?" I say to Jane when we're outside the bar next door to the hotel.

"Yes."

"Then c'mon." On the two thousand pound bull, I was calm and collected. But now that I'm back in Jane's presence, I'm nervous.

"I thought we—"

"Oh, we are." I take her hand and lead her toward the parking garage instead of the hotel entrance. Jane Harper—or whoever she really is—has rattled me to the core. I've always thought the thrill and terror of mounting a raging beast with the ability to end my life in seconds would make me feel the most alive. But I was wrong.

This woman, blindly trusting me as I lead her to my truck, makes me feel things I've never experienced before. It's like part of me was dormant before I met her, and I don't want our first time to be in some cliché hotel room.

"Where are we going?" she asks.

I open the passenger door and help her inside the truck, unable to keep my hands from grazing the sides of her tits. "Have you ever laid out under the stars in the back of a pickup?"

A twinkle dances in her eyes. "No."

"Well, that's where we're going." Away from the fans, away from the after party, away from the city. I want to show her what makes my heart happy. I don't want this weekend to be the last time I see Jane. I want it to be the first. But I have to know she can be happy living on a quiet ranch.

Holding her hand, I drive us a couple of miles outside of town until I find a dark, private country road.

"Where did you get the blankets?" she asks as I spread a couple of comforters in the bed of the truck.

"Not important." The hotel might send me a bill for them, but I don't care. Every dollar this costs me will be worth it. "Climb on up." I help her onto the tailgate of the truck. She dangles her feet. The moonlight reveals her biting that damn lip again. Fuck, it makes me crazy.

I step between her legs and draw her in for the kiss I've been thinking of nonstop since I had to say goodbye to her before the show. Our tongues mingle hungrily. I find her tits again and squeeze them through the blouse.

The urgency between us grows quickly. I no longer have the patience to undo individual buttons. "It's a cheap shirt," she tells me. So I rip it open instead. Her lace bra is on full display. I admire the way her tits fill it out only moments before I undo the clasp.

She moans as I take one nipple into my mouth, then the other. "Fuck, these are beautiful."

"You like them?"

I growl against her nipple. "You know I do."

She tugs at my belt, undoing all my plans. "I've been thinking about this all day, Colt." Once my zipper is undone, she shimmies back onto the pile of blankets sans shirt and bra in invitation. The moonlight illuminates her naked top, calling me like a siren. I shed my shirt and crawl onto the bed.

"Let's get you out of these jeans."

"Please!"

I slide her jeans over her hips, exposing a pair of panties that matches her bra. I tease her pussy through the lace fabric with my fingers. "You're so wet, babe."

"It's what you do to me, cowboy."

My dick hardens the rest of the way at that declaration. The desire in her eyes begs me to pleasure her in every way possible. "Just wait until you see what else I'm going to do to you."

5

SONYA

Colt hovers his mouth above my panty-covered pussy and teases me with his hot breath. My nipples ache with want, and I'm unable to fight the urge to rock my hips into his face. His lips collide with the lace.

"These need to go," he says.

Time is an illusion, because it feels like only a second passes from wearing panties to not having them on at all. His tongue strokes my swollen bud in slow circles. "That feels so *good*, Colt." I'm not completely inexperienced, but I've never let a man go down on me before.

I've never been brave enough. But Jane Harper *is* brave. I like her. I like her *a lot*.

"You taste so delicious." His mouth works magic on my drenched pussy. I'm feeling dizzy when one finger enters me, then two. He strokes his fingers in and out as his mouth covers my clit. The mixture of sensations is an overwhelming wave of pleasure, and I hope I never come down from it.

"Fuck, Colt!" I cry out, loving the fact that we're out in the middle of nowhere so I can be as loud as I want to. And with everything this cowboy is making me feel, I don't care to be a bit quiet.

I rock my hips against his hungry mouth until I'm taken completely over the edge. I cry out his name. I see stars—and not the ones overhead.

"You like that, huh?" he says with a sexy smirk.

"Oh yeah."

I'm panting heavily and still recovering from the epic orgasm I never knew was possible. I don't know why I waited so long to let a man suck my cunt but I won't make that mistake again. Except, I only want Colt's mouth down there. Is it possible that I'm starting to fall for this cowboy?

Colt slips off his jeans, but before he can climb on top of me, I sit up. If I was plain Sonya, I might not have the courage to do what I'm about to do. But as Jane and the way Colt's eyes rake over my body like it's a decadent dessert, I have an overabundance of confidence.

"On your back, cowboy."

The hungry gleam in his gaze makes my nipples

ache for this touch. I'm not some skinny model, and I'm not used to a man being so fiercely drawn to me.

"You comfortable?" I ask him, practically panting at the sight of his hard shaft ready for my pussy. I should be worried it won't fit, but I know it will.

"I am."

"Good. It's my turn to ride something tonight." I lower my hips and guide his cock to my entrance. I stroke the head of dick along my wet folds, coating him in my juices. "I'm clean," I tell him.

"Me too." His gaze flickers away, then back. "I haven't been with a woman in years."

My heart thrums in my chest at that confession. "You probably say that to all the pretty girls."

"It's the truth. You're the first woman who's turned my head in a long time."

With our gazes trapped together, I feel like this might be the time to confess my little secret. But I'm terrified the truth will change his mind about me. All day, he's been getting to know Jane Harper, romance author. I'm not ready to lose him to the boring Sonya Williamson. Not yet.

"I don't make a habit of riding cowboys," I tell him. "Or… any man."

"Good. Because I don't have any intention of sharing you." He shackles his hands on my hips and helps me lower onto his cock. I gasp as he fills me, relishing in the feel of him inside me. I feel… complete. "I want you all to myself."

"I'm all yours."

With his hands to guide me, I gyrate on top of him. "There you go, babe." I slide slowly onto his cock and quickly release until just his head hovers at my center. Together, we find a rhythm that perfectly pleasures and tortures both of us.

"Fuck, Colt." I'm whimpering it feels so good. I drop my pussy until I feel his balls against my skin. With him seated deep inside, I rock my hips, rubbing my clit against him.

"That's it, Jane. I want you to come on my dick."

The dirty words sound so sexy with his deep voice. It's a command I can't help but obey. I increase my speed until I feel that wave of pleasure sweep over me. Just as I start to shutter an orgasm, Colt grips my hips tighter and thrusts into me with such force I might actually split in two.

"Come inside me, Colt." And he does. Everything is right with the world in this moment.

COLT

"Stay with me tonight," I ask Jane once I park the truck back in the parking garage.

"Colt, I—"

"Please, Jane."

"Okay."

I can't imagine spending another day away from this woman. I've never felt so complete inside someone before. Though there are certainly a lot of mysteries about her, I want to learn them all. Starting tonight with her in my arms, in my bed. Preferably naked.

My cock is already half-hard at the thought of another round of pleasure.

"Just let me text my friend so she doesn't worry."

"Of course."

I lead her to my room, unable to keep my hands off of her. Simply touching this woman makes my entire body ignite with life. Once I shut the door, I draw her in for the most sensual kiss we've shared. It's not the greedy, hungry kisses of before. It's filled with hope and promise.

"Colt, there's something I need to tell you."

The alarm bells from earlier start to sound again, but I block them out. I kiss her neck, slowly. I want her, again—I think that'll always be the case—but this time, I want to memorize every inch of her body. I want to worship her in a way no one has or ever will again. "Later, babe."

I slip her shirt off her shoulders easily enough since all but one button was lost in the passionate tumble earlier. "Tell me, Jane. Where are you from?"

"Here," she says in a breathy whisper.

I'm surprised by her answer, but don't stop my

mission to kiss every inch of skin. I slip her bra off next. Her nipples are already standing at attention, begging for my touch. I'll never get tired of this.

"What do you do?" I ask, working my tongue down to her nipple. "Other than write?" If she's not published, it stands to reason she has another job. All details I need to sort out if I'm going to figure out how to make this work.

"In between jobs—" She moans when I gently bite her nipple. "—at the moment."

I unbutton her jeans and slowly roll them down her hips. "Do you like the city?"

"It's okay."

Good. I can work with that. "How do you feel about the country?"

"After tonight?" Her laugh is full of naughty desire. I'd bet my season earnings on it. "I'm a fan."

I slip my hand down her panties, and it takes only half a second to discover she's wet and ready for me again. I slowly stroke that swollen bud, loving the sexy moans that escape her perfect lips.

"Ever ridden a horse?" I ask.

"Nope."

"That's okay." I plunge a finger inside her hot channel. "I can teach you."

I kiss her when she moans again. We're not out in the middle of nowhere this time, and if she gets any louder there'll be banging on the walls. I love that she's so unguarded, but I can respect the fact that we currently have neighbors.

"Do you have any family here?" This question causes a slight quiver of fear to race through me. Family is everything to me. If I had to leave them behind to follow a woman, I would live to resent it. I could never ask that of someone else.

"No. Just Jillian."

"Your friend?"

"Yep."

She's apparently too lost in a pleasure-filled hazed to realize her slip-up. She's just given away the secret identity of her best friend. It's almost not fair of me to ask, but I do anyway. I have to know. "What's your real name, Jane?"

"Sonya."

I lead her to the bed, lowering her down onto the mattress. I slip off her panties before undressing myself. "Lay down, Sonya." Her name—her *real* name—feels good on my lips. "I'm going to worship every inch of your beautiful body."

Sonya Wilder. The name has a nice ring to it.

6

SONYA

The next morning, I feel happy. So damn happy. I'm sore in all the best ways, and I wouldn't change a single thing that happened last night. It makes me think that maybe I *do* need to try my hand at a romance novel. Because Jane Harper is exactly the kickass woman I want to be.

"Thinking about your book?" Colt asks beside me in the booth. We opted out of a hotel breakfast, certain we'd be inundated by the romance writers. Colt didn't want the attention, and I secretly didn't want to risk being outed by *Darla*. We narrowly escaped her when we left. I brought Colt to one of my favorite breakfast spots—their pancakes are the best kept secret in town.

"You could say that."

Colt fishes a finger at the safety pin I've used in place of the top button of my blouse. "We could've stopped by your room you know."

"You do not want to be the one who wakes up Jillian unannounced." That part is true—my bestie turns into an all-out fighter who swings first and asks questions later. I have a string of texts to read from her—apparently, she did not go straight home when Colt and I left the bar. But I'll read those later.

At least for the morning, I want to enjoy Colt's company. I want to pretend that he's not going to drive away tomorrow, never to be seen again. His next rodeo is five hundred miles away, or I'd go.

"What's that frown about?" He lifts my chin with a finger and places a gentle kiss on my still swollen lips.

"You must travel a lot," I say.

"More weekends than not," he admits.

Last night he peppered me with several questions. Now, it's my turn. "Where do you live? When you're not on the road?"

"Montana."

Immediately, I picture mountains, ranches that go on for miles, and calm. I've never lived anywhere but here. Honking horns and sirens are noises I've learned to tune out. But it doesn't mean I enjoy them. "That sounds wonderful."

As the server takes our order, I let myself fantasize about living on a quiet ranch. Married to Colt. Maybe even writing a real novel. The only thing I have keeping me here is Jillian. I'd hate to leave my best friend, though. She's the reason I even met Colt.

"Do you live with your brothers?"

"We share a ranch, but we all have separate houses." Colt tucks a lock of hair behind my ear and kisses me softly on that tender spot just below my lobe. "Any more questions?"

"What do—"

"Jane Harper?" Darla's nasally, shrill voice echoes in the restaurant, causing me to cringe and panic in the same moment.

"That's me."

Darla—still in that blue vest—has one hand on her hip and the other waving a clipboard. Does the woman seriously not travel without it? "I looked you up, Jane Harper. You're not a published author."

"I know that."

"Darla," Colt says in that suave, sexy voice that caused more than half the authors to swoon yesterday, "We're trying to enjoy a nice breakfast. Can this wait?"

"No, I'm afraid it cannot!"

Fear pricks my chest. I don't know what I did to make this woman target me—well, other than breaking and entering her private pre-rodeo event without an invitation. My eyes wildly scan the restaurant for cops. Maybe I'm going to get arrested after all. I'll kill Jillian if that happens.

"Then please make this quick."

"Only *published* authors are allowed at this convention. And I looked you up. Not a single published title under Jane Harper. Or Mandi Flowers."

Colt's warm fingers caress my bare shoulder, but I can sense the uneasy tension. He's about to find out just how unexciting my real identity is. Because *Darla* here is not budging. With a deep breath, I muster the courage to rip off the Band-Aid before this gets any worse.

"I'm not a published author," I admit.

"I knew it!"

I peel my narrowed eyes from Darla and look at Colt instead. He's the one who needs to know the truth. If there's even a tiny beacon of hope that we'll have a future together, this lie can't go on any longer. "I'm not writing a book, Colt. I'm not even a writer."

"Aha!"

I shoot daggers at Darla with my death glare. "You can *go* now." I don't know if it's the force in my tone or the menacing stare, but Darla finally backs away. She fiddles with her clipboard all the way to her corner booth.

"You're not a writer?" There's an edge of disappointment or hurt in his voice, I'm just not sure which.

"No." I take a gulp of ice water and continue. "My real name is Sonya Williamson. I got laid off from my cubicle job yesterday." I add in the details about the flat tire, spilled coffee, and splash of mud. "Jillian wanted to make me feel better, so we crashed the pre-rodeo event and pretended to be authors."

I take a deep breath and hold in the air as I anxiously await his reaction. Twice he parts his lips to say something, but doesn't.

"I'm sorry I lied, Colt. I thought…I thought after the weekend was over that I'd never see you again. I like Jane Harper. She has more confidence in her pinky finger that Sonya has in her entire body. It was nice to feel like I was somebody."

Colt drops his arm from around my shoulders, and I feel my heart sink into the pit of stomach.

"I was going to tell you—"

"Were you, though?" He slides out of the booth, dropping a twenty on the table. The wounded look in his cobalt eyes cracks me right in two. I should've told him before we ever went inside that RV.

"Colt—"

"I'm sorry. I need to go."

For the first time since her invention, I wish I could erase Jane Harper from existence.

7

COLT

Hours later, my mind still races wildly. I've done everything I can think of to erase Jane—*Sonya*—from my mind. I need to focus on my job, which is to stay on that bull for eight seconds. But right now, I don't think I could stay on the back of a sheep, much less an angry bull. I've never been rattled like this before.

Maybe there's a reason I've kept my distance from women. They're distracting and nothing but trouble.

"You look mad enough to punch a bull in the face and not regret it." Hudson takes a seat next to me on the empty stands, handing me a bottle of water. Though my brother likes to pretend he doesn't have a heart, deep down I know the man has one made of gold.

"Thanks." I uncap the bottle and down half of it.

"So what's up?"

"Nothing."

"Liar."

I empty the rest of the bottle, then squeeze the plastic until it's a shriveled mess in my hands. Just like my mind is right now. "How do you do it?"

"Do what?"

"Fall for a different woman every weekend and still manage to win most of the time?"

"Ah, so this is about *her*."

"Doesn't matter." I hop up from the stands, unwilling to talk about the woman who shimmied her way into my heart. She lied about being a writer. *What else did she lie about?*

"Of course, it does."

"She *lied* to me, Hudson. That's all there is to it."

He follows me as I march back to the area behind the grandstands. I don't have much time before the gates open and they start letting fans in. I don't want to be anywhere near people tonight. I'm going to draw my bull, do my ride, and spend every other minute hiding out in Uncle Raine's RV.

"If that was it, you wouldn't be so upset."

I round on him before I reach the gate. "Stop, please."

Hudson lifts both hands in surrender. "If that's

what you want, then fine. But you and I both know you can't ride a bull for shit with a clogged-up head."

"I'll ride just fine."

"Wanna make a bet?"

My world spins beneath my feet, and if I couldn't see Hudson standing there without a problem, I might think there was an earthquake. *The bet.* "If it weren't for your stupid bet, I never would've met her."

"You're welcome."

"Forget punching a bull—"

"Think about it, Colt. I've never seen you hung up on a woman before. Really *think.*" Hudson trots off before I can get in any more jabs or spew any more harsh words. He's really a pretty great brother. Austin and Tex are great too, but I've always been closest with Hudson. It's the only reason he tolerated me just now.

So I do what he suggests, despite how much I don't want to. I *think*.

Memories from the past twenty-four hours flood my mind. The first time I spotted Sonya in the stands. The way she felt with my arm around her as her friend snapped a dozen pictures. That sizzling kiss in the RV. The way the moonlight bathed her naked body in a soft glow. Her giggle as she scrounged up safety pins to fix the shirt I ripped open last night.

Maybe her name was a lie, but the chemistry

between us wasn't fabricated. That much I know. I can't deny that my heart still wants her—no matter what her real name is.

I think some more, on the words she said to me this morning. How Jane Harper was the brave one, not Sonya. "But she *was* being brave." Standing up to Darla. Telling me the truth. She had a crappy day and found a way to overcome it.

I feel like a giant jackass.

I'm about to jump in my truck and rush back to the hotel to find her—*if* she's even staying there. But I hear a call over the louder speaker for all riders to report. It's our safety brief that'll be followed by drawing our bulls. Missing that means disqualification.

"Shit," I mutter.

SONYA

"This is a terrible idea," I say to Jillian. We're once again at the rodeo, even using the VIP tickets Colt acquired for us. This is the *last* place we should be.

"This is the perfect solution."

"I don't see your vision," I say flatly. I scan the area, like I have been every two minutes, looking for Colt. It's stupid, but I can't help it. If we were anywhere else, I could forget about him so much easier.

"Your cowboy will see you, and how he reacts will tell you everything you need to know." I narrow my eyes at Jillian, set on lighting her on fire with my glare. But through my misplaced annoyance, I see the glow in my best friend.

"Wait, what have *you* been keeping from *me*?"

"We'll talk about it later. Right now, this is about you."

Despite my curiosity, I don't have the energy to extract Jillian's secret. So I go back to brooding. "He's not going to be happy to see me."

"You don't know that." Jillian snakes an arm around my shoulders and squeezes me against her. "He's had some time to clear his head. If he's really the man you say he is, he'll come around."

The announcer starts the show, and the crowd around us erupts. I manage a couple of weak, unenthusiastic claps. He introduces the riders, same as last night, and I wait to hear Colt's name. But I don't.

"Sonya." I'm sure I imagined that smooth, sexy voice. The crowd is loud, and my heart is in shreds. It has to be the delusions of a desperate woman. Maybe I don't write romance novels, but dammit, I was certainly happy living in one.

"Hey," says Jillian.

"I'm fine. Just ignore me."

Jillian shoves at my shoulder. "You have a visitor."

Colt steps in front of me, blocking the view. Because there are three other rows behind us, he quickly takes a knee. "I've been looking for you *everywhere*." He's panting, like he's been running.

"Why isn't your name on the board?" It's the dumbest question I could ask, considering the man I thought I lost for good is kneeling before me.

"I'm disqualified."

"What?"

"I missed the draw."

"You didn't. You wouldn't—"

"I'm an ass. I'm sorry I left you in the restaurant."

My heart stutters in my chest, and I think I might cry. I'm scared and relieved and cautious, and my stupid emotions can't handle feeling everything at once. "I'm sorry I lied, Colt."

"I know why you did."

"I'm not a writer. I mean, maybe someday—"

"You don't have to write a romance novel, babe. Just come make one with me."

Breath halts in my lungs as I'm sure I've heard him wrong. "But the event—"

"Losing you would be worse than any disqualification. I love you, Sonya. I know it's fast, but I've never felt this connected to anyone in my entire life. I have to have you. The thought of you with some other guy makes me crazy. You belong with me. Only me."

I cradle his face with my hands, desperate to kiss him. It feels like weeks have passed since our lips met, not hours. "You really love me?"

"Yes, I do."

"I'm glad it's not just me then." I do kiss him then, not holding back despite the glares from some of the romance writers nearby, including Darla. "I love you, too, Colt. It doesn't make any sense to me—it all happened so fast. I guess when you know, you know."

"Say you'll come back to Montana with me. Let's create our happily ever after."

I glance at Jillian, the only tie I have keeping me here. I'll miss her…

"If you don't say yes," Jillian says, "I'll tie you up in the trunk of my car and drive you there myself." I have the greatest best friend in the world.

"Yes, Colt. Let's do this."

EPILOGUE

COLT

It's been two blissful years since I first asked Sonya to move to Montana with me. Every day I'm certain things can't get better, but they do.

"It looks like rain," she says to me, stepping off the porch hesitantly in her boots. The best decision I ever made was buying her that pair of cowgirl boots. She looks so damn sexy in them.

I draw her into my embrace and give her a kiss that leaves us both gasping for air. She's bravest when she's a little lightheaded. "You're getting on the horse, babe."

"I don't know about this..."

"You've ridden me plenty of times. I promise, Butterscotch is much easier. Less *bumpy*." She bites that bottom lip, a flash of desire dancing across her eyes. It's been two crazy years with Sonya traveling with me to most of the events. She even started writing a romance novel, but she won't let me read it yet.

"*Not* the same thing."

"I'm retiring at the end of the season. We're going to ride horses together. *A lot*."

"Then I'll try when the season's over."

"Summon your inner Jane Harper and get your cute ass on this horse." The words are as effective as Hudson convincing me to make a bet. Sonya approaches the horse with a new found bravery.

"You're lucky I love you, Colt Wilder."

I help her onto Butterscotch, not shy at all about grabbing her ass as it lifts into the air. I have plans for her tonight, and all of them involve the two of us naked and starting a family. "Not as lucky as I am to have you as my wife."

HUDSON

WILDER BROTHERS RODEO BOOK 2

1

JILLIAN

The only thing trickier than sneaking *into* a private event uninvited is sneaking out.

Sure, I could follow the herd of romance authors through the main gate, but I'd have to face Darla, the organizer, again. She's already onto me and my bestie Sonya. She doesn't believe we're romance authors who are part of her convention weekend.

For the record, she's right.

But I'm not about to give her the satisfaction of proving it.

I don't know about Sonya, but I've never written a word in my life that I wasn't forced to. But my ability to think on the fly was on point today. That's the only way I was able to invent pen names for the both of us so quickly so we would blend in.

I slip behind the stands and search for that hole in the fence, leaving Sonya with her hot cowboy tour guide. I was hoping to cheer her up after her horrible day, but she may have hit the jackpot. No way I would intrude on their *private* tour.

Crashing this exclusive rodeo gathering for romance writers was the most obvious cure for my bestie's bad day. A hot, suave cowboy can cure anything. Judging by the lustful twinkle in Sonya's eyes when I left her alone with the bull rider Colt Wilder, I'm right.

"Going somewhere?"

I freeze in my tracks, and my breath hitches. Shit, I've been caught.

"Looking for something I dropped," I say to the male voice coming from somewhere behind my left shoulder. I don't dare look. It might be that incredibly sexy cowboy I saw lingering off to the side earlier. *Hudson Wilder*. The bronc rider. A brother to the cowboy I left Sonya with. I may have Googled him. A few times.

I begin searching the ground for the mystery thing I dropped, hoping he'll just go and leave me to it.

I was interested—at first. But I saw him flirting with a couple of the rodeo girls in those Daisy Duke shorts. Super skinny and wavy hair down to their tiny little butts. And some of the posts I found on social media painted a pretty clear picture. Yeah, no thanks. I'm never going to be in a magazine or anything, but I love my curves. And I don't have time for a womanizer who thinks he's the greatest gift to women since cherry lip gloss.

"What did you drop?" His smooth voice sends shivers throughout my body, no matter how much I fight it.

"My necklace."

"But you're wearing one."

It's time to turn around and face him. Even from a distance earlier, I could tell those eyes could melt panties. It's like all those movies where they tell people to cover their eyes and don't look. I'm about to be the receiver of some terrible curse that can never be undone.

"I dropped a second one. Had it in my pocket."

"What does it look like?"

I bite down on my bottom lip, fighting to maintain control. But my gaze rakes over the sinfully hot cowboy. In his relaxed T-shirt and Wranglers, the amount of muscle he's sporting is very apparent. Stubble dusts his chin and cheeks, and I yearn to run my fingers over it. Dammit, this is hard.

"You know, maybe I left it in the hotel room after all."

"I can help you look."

I gulp when the scent of his cologne drifts to me. Dammit, he even *smells* sexy. "Really not necessary."

"If you're sure."

"I'm sure."

Hudson takes a stride closer to me, leaving us mere inches apart. In the shaded area behind the stands, the heat swirling between the very small gap is undeniable. Very naughty thoughts dance through my overactive imagination. I need to get away.

"Thanks, though." My voice is so quiet, I'm not even sure he heard me.

"I know you're not a romance writer."

My heart races at the conviction in his voice. "Of course I am. I'm Mandi Flowers." The lie doesn't do anything to relax that intense gaze of his. My traitorous nipples turn to pebbles beneath my lace bra. "I wr—write vampire ones."

Hudson leans a little closer, his lips a breath away from my ear. A sensible person would run or at least scream for help with a stranger this close. But that's never been me. Nope. "Prove it."

HUDSON

"I don't need to prove it." The fiery blonde going by the fake pen name Mandi Flowers takes a step back.

But it's a tiny step that tells me I have her snared in my trap.

I'm not going to lie, I've always had a way with women. They're drawn to me, much like the rodeo girls earlier during Colt's presentation. I never entertain their interest beyond conversation, but if you ask any one of my brothers or the media, they'd label me a womanizer.

"You can't prove it, babe. Because you're not really a writer."

Her gaze flickers to the fence, near the same spot I watched her and her friend sneak in from earlier. I could've turned them in, but I really wanted to see how it was all going to play out. Even from a distance, I could tell the woman standing before me now was the instigator.

"You know this because you read loads of romance novels, huh?" She fidgets with her necklace —I know there isn't a second one.

The breeze lifts a lock of hair, fluttering it in front of her crystal blue eyes. I catch it with my fingers and leisurely tuck it behind her ear. "I Googled Mandi Flowers. No results."

"I'm not published yet."

I'll give this woman credit. She doesn't back down. "If Darla knew that, she wouldn't have invited you along. Today's behind the scenes tour was for *published* romance authors only." I only know this because originally, I was selected to entertain the private group. But Colt lost a bet to me. That left me on the sidelines to enjoy his discomfort.

"She made an exception for me."

Almost as if it were orchestrated, the gaggle of authors strolls by on the sidewalk on the opposite side of the fence. "Mind if I confirm that?" I manage a single step before her hands shackle my arm and yank me back.

"Okay, okay. So I'm *not* an author." She stretches onto her toes to peer over my shoulder. "Just please don't rat me out."

I have no intention of outing her little secret. Colt seems very smitten with her friend—and he's never smitten with anyone. I'm not about to spoil that. But I do quite enjoy riling this woman up. "Then tell me your real name."

"What?"

"That's not a hard question to answer."

"You don't need to know—" One glance over my shoulder is all it takes for her to relent. "Fine, fine. My name is Jillian. Happy?"

"Almost."

Jillian lets out a heavy sigh, but she doesn't do a thing to put any real distance between us. I could draw her into my arms with little effort at our proximity. Devour that pretty mouth in one sweeping motion.

"Look, I'm not interested."

I purposely drop my gaze to her tits. Her hard

nipples poke through the thin fabric of her tank top. "Is that so?"

"I don't get tangled up with players. And you most definitely are a player."

"Actually, I'm not." Though toying with her has been incredibly entertaining, I hope she can hear the sincerity in my voice now. I fear she's had a chance to see what they say about me online.

"Oh yeah? Prove it."

I reach out my hand, palm up, in offering. "C'mon on, then."

"What are you doing?"

"I'm going to prove to you that I'm not the ladies' man everyone paints me out to be. But you'll have to spend the day with me to see it."

Her blue eyes stare at my hand for several seconds, and I find for the first time, I'm nervous I'm about to be shot down. It's not something I'm used to, and I don't care for how it feels. The churning of my stomach, the tightening in my chest. I realize I'm more drawn to this woman than I've ever been drawn to anyone.

I'm not about to let her walk away now that I've met her.

After what feels like hours, Jillian drops her hand into mine. "Fine. Let's see what you're all about, cowboy."

2

JILLIAN

"Where are we going?" I ask.

He flashes me that pleasure inducing smile, causing a series of tingles between my thighs. I cross my legs. "Patience. It's not far away."

I should've turned Hudson down, for several reasons. One, I know a womanizer when I see one. The man will use all that cowboy charm to try and convince me otherwise, but I'm not stupid. I've encountered his kind before.

Second, I'm supposed to be hanging for sale signs and lockboxes right now on three different properties. I left the office and never told my boss I'd be taking a few hours off to soothe my bestie. To be fair, he already left for the weekend. Probably off with some hot date—womanizer example number one. But I *am* supposed to be working.

Add to that list that Hudson is a stranger and I'm now driving toward the city limits in his truck without telling anyone ... I know better.

Yet here I am.

"Do I get any hints?"

"It's the closest I can get to being in my natural element, other than the arena."

That doesn't give me much to go on, but I doubt he's about to give me more clues than that. So I change tactics. "You're a bronc rider?"

"Yes."

"Why not bulls?"

Hudson lets out an easy, unguarded laugh that I know is not for my benefit. I relax, just a little. It will take a whole lot more than that, though, for me to let my defenses down. "I'm better on a horse, and they don't have horns."

"This rodeo thing is a family thing?"

"Yep. You met Colt, he's the bull rider. Then you got Austin and Tex."

"They ride too?"

"Austin is a pickup man. Tex is always in the ring, distracting a mad animal when it's set on crushing a few bones."

I wish I knew more about the rodeo, but to be

honest, I've never been to one. The private tour Sonya and I crashed is the closest I've ever come. So these descriptions don't mean much to me, but I'm too embarrassed to ask.

I will admit, I've always had a thing for a man in a cowboy hat, though. That's probably how I ended up in a truck headed out of the city limits and into the country with a complete stranger. "You're not an axe murderer, right Hudson Wilder?"

He slows the truck and turns onto a dirt path off the highway. "No, ma'am."

The way he says *ma'am* makes my nipples tighten. It's so fucking sexy and smooth. I remind myself that he could still be a player. That giving into him might be playing right in his hands and utterly stupid. But the longer I'm alone with him, the harder it is to keep this logic rooted in my brain. "You're sure? Because I see an awful lot of woods around here."

He slows the truck and parks. Leaning over the center console, he looks me straight in the eyes. "I promise, you're safe with me." The sincerity and conviction in his tone thrills me, and my guard slips a little more.

"Where are we?"

"A friend's ranch."

"A friend?" I quirk an eyebrow at that. I don't know where Hudson Wilder calls home, but if it were here, I'd know about it. Our small city isn't big enough for someone like him to blend in unnoticed.

"My brothers and I have traveled all over, and we've made some friends in different places. This is one of them."

Finally able to tear my eyes away from Hudson and shake away the naughty thoughts forming in my overactive imagination, I take a closer look at where we are. A barn sits off to one side. A two-story house with a covered porch is laid out in front of us. A fence stretches between the two, enclosing half a dozen horses.

Before I can ask who this *friend* is, a woman appears on the porch. At first glance, a surge of jealousy fills me. She's gorgeous with her auburn hair, big smile, and cowgirl boots. She's skinny in all the ways I am not.

"This is Natalie. She's like a second mom to me."

Squinting my eyes through the windshield, it's easier to see her age now. My jealousy meter eases up.

"C'mon. I want to introduce you."

"If it isn't the famous Hudson Wilder." Natalie hops off the porch and swings her arms around Hudson. It's easy to see they're old friends, and at this closer range, there's not a trace of lust in Natalie's eyes. I finally relax.

"Natalie, I want you to meet my friend Jillian."

"It's a pleasure." Before I can extend a hand out, I'm trapped in a hug of my own. "Sorry, sugar. I'm a hugger." Finally, she lets goes so I can refill my lungs with oxygen. For such a petite woman, she's certainly strong. "Hudson, you've never brought anyone over for me to meet before. Is there something you want to tell me?"

Heat flares up through my neck and settles onto my rosy cheeks. I turn toward the barn, hopeful to hide my embarrassment. How's he going to explain bringing a woman he *just* met? At the same time, I'm relieved no other girl has ever earned an introduction to Natalie before, as she's obviously someone important in his life.

Hudson gives her a wink, but his gaze settles on me as he says, "Not yet."

"I know you can't stay for supper with the rodeo tonight, but can I fix you two anything to eat now?"

"Actually, I was hoping we could borrow your barn."

"Go for it," Natalie says with a wave. "I'll be inside if you need me."

My eyebrows shoot clear up to my hairline, and I swallow hard. What would two people with an obvious burning attraction need with a barn? I should hightail it out of here, but it's too late for me to run away. There's a roguish side of me that doesn't want to anyway.

HUDSON

The first moment I spotted Jillian dragging her friend through a gap in the fence, I was intrigued. I suspected even then that she wasn't really a romance writer. But I wasn't going to spoil her fun. I kept off to the sidelines, pretending to watch my brother squirm in front of an audience. But really, I wanted to watch Jillian.

When the two rodeo girls came up to chat, I didn't want to be rude. Rude is not in my nature. But I made it clear I wasn't interested, even after they begged me to join them at the after party tonight. I usually make an appearance at those things, but if I go tonight, it will be with Jillian on my arm or not at all.

But of course Jillian had spotted the interaction and no doubt formed the same conclusion so many others do when I'm bombarded by women.

"Why are we going to the barn?" Jillian asks as she walks beside me.

"I want to show you something. You'll see."

"If it's full of a bunch of things with rusty blades, I'm out. I'm not going out in some horror movie fashion."

I take her hand, unable to contain my laughter. "I

promise I'm not going to murder you." I'd never hurt her. I'd do anything necessary to protect her, and if anyone dared try to cause her harm, they'd answer to me.

The powerful pull I feel to Jillian is sudden. I've never experienced anything in my life like it before. But deep down in my gut, I know I was meant to find her. It's been too easy to imagine a future together—lazy days on the front porch watching the sunset, sipping coffee in the morning, tumbling naked between the sheets. I want it all.

Jillian takes a cautious step into the barn. But the most frightening object inside is an old pitchfork. Or maybe it's Earl, the grumpy old cow who doesn't really like the outdoors. But he's penned up in a corner. He won't bother us.

"What is this place?"

"Natalie's from a rodeo family, too. Her family and mine were close, back when my dad ran the circuit. Whenever we were down this way, we always stayed on this ranch." I lead Jillian to the practice barrel, happy to see that it's still set up just like I remembered.

"Why is there a barrel floating in the air?"

I take her hand and spin her around to face me. "You can read all the articles and social media posts about me you want, and they'll all say the same thing. But I want to show you a part of who I really am. A part I don't share with anyone."

"And that includes a floating barrel?"

It's impossible not to laugh around Jillian. It makes my soul feel complete, somehow. I don't know how I'm going to make a future work with her, but I'll figure it out. I have to. This woman belongs with me. I've never been more certain of anything.

3

JILLIAN

"You haven't answered my question." I point to the barrel suspended by four different ropes. If I'm not mistaken, there's some kind of padding on the top to replicate a saddle. It's strapped to the barrel with heavy duty tape. "You—you don't want me to get on that, do you?"

Hudson removes his hat and places it on my head. "Where's your sense of adventure?"

My nipples ache at this point. They're painfully desperate for his touch. All the way out in the country, away from reality, it's easy to pretend that there's only Hudson and me. That maybe, just maybe, he could be a one-woman kind of guy. I'm so close to falling for that trap.

"Does this simulate riding a horse?"

"Bronc. Or bull. Works for both."

I get motion sickness in a canoe. "I'm not getting on that thing."

"I'll be right here the whole time." The fierce reassurance in his eyes causes my heart to pound in my ears. I want to kiss him. Badly.

But there's still a sensible part of me that knows climbing onto a barrel suspended by four measly pieces of rope might not be the wisest decision I ever make. I'm not exactly light as a feather. "I don't think I should."

Hudson's fingers brush along my cheek, turning my face up toward his. "Trust me, Jillian."

"If I fall off this thing—" *or cause the damn thing to snap a rope,* "—this date is over."

"We're on a date?"

I push playfully at his shoulder, forcing the desperately needed distance between us. "You know what I mean." That low, rumbling laughter is going to be the death of me. It's already the end of these panties for as soaked through as they are.

"Let me help you up."

I want to object, but the barrel comes up to the top of my hip. I'd make a fool of myself trying to mount that thing on my own. Plus, I'm a little giddy at the thought of Hudson's hands on me. I'm starting to care just a little less about his player status. Maybe I'm the one who's too uptight.

He lifts me onto the barrel like it's nothing. Like I'm light as air. His hands slowly slide from my back, and I think he might kiss me now. Our lips are hardly inches apart. But he steps away toward one of the front ropes and grabs it with his hand.

"Now, you have to do this the right way. One hand under the rope, the other up in the air."

"I'm supposed to stay on this thing one-handed?"

"That's the rules. You use two hands, you get disqualified."

I'm still not ready to admit I've never been to a rodeo. Sonya's cowboy already promised us VIP tickets for tonight's show, so I'm sure this little barrel ride will all make more sense in a few hours.

"Hold on," Hudson says. "You have to counter your body when the barrel moves." He gently tugs on the rope, pulling the barrel forward. I'm not ready and my body lurches for the front of the barrel. My breasts brush the cold metal, but I manage to right myself quickly. I'm no quitter.

"Try it again."

This time, I'm ready when he tugs on the rope. I rock my body the opposite direction, keeping my hand in the air. His smile alone makes me feel like a champion barrel rider. I'm sure it's a thing. At least, in my imagination it is. And I hope Hudson is first prize.

"You're doing great, Jilly."

In my ornery tone, I say, "This doesn't seem so hard after all."

Hudson yanks harder on the rope this time, and I almost lose my balance. But I squeeze my thighs tight against the barrel and hang on for dear life. "I can up the difficultly level at any time," he says.

I almost ask him what else I could ride, but I catch myself before that bold statement slips out. Though I've literally thought of nothing else but getting naked with Hudson since we entered the barn, I'm not about to admit that to him.

HUDSON

"You're a natural," I say to Jillian as I help her off the barrel. I know she could slide down on her own without difficulty, but I want the excuse to slide my hands up her sides. Her tits brush against my chest as I lift her.

"That was fun," she says to me.

I should take a step back, create a small barrier of distance between us. But I don't want to. My gaze keeps dropping to her lips, then her tits. This woman has me so riled up, it'll be a miracle if I can keep my head clear enough to ride eight seconds later tonight.

"Do I get a prize or something?" she teases, her eyes darkened by the desire we both feel. "I didn't fall off."

I have to kiss her. It's the only hope I have.

Pulling her into my embrace, I drop my lips to hers hungrily, tasting cherry lip gloss. Our mouths fuse together in a passionate exploration. My hands comb over her perfect curves until they reach her ass. I yank her against me, wanting her to feel what this one kiss is doing to me.

The primal side of me longs to take her right here in this barn. But the reasonable side of me knows she'll never believe I'm not some player if I do.

"Wow," she pants when our lips momentarily break apart. We're both a little winded from the experience, and I don't know about Jillian, but my legs are unsteady.

"Wow is right." I pull her back against me by the beltloops of her jeans and slide my hands beneath her loose shirt. We should stop, because the further I go, the less control I'll have to do just that. But I can't. I've longed for Jillian all my life, but I never knew it until I met her today.

She wraps her hands around the back of my neck and drags me down for another round of steamy kissing as my hands work their way to her lacy bra. I can feel her hardened nipples beneath the thin fabric and I give them a squeeze.

Jillian moans against my mouth.

Greedily I work at the clasp of her bra until it pops free, allowing my hands to slide beneath it easily. Her tits feel amazing in my hands. I want to taste them. Suckle them. I want her to moan my name with that sexy, sweet voice of hers.

I lift her shirt, exposing her erect nipples. Pushing the bra out of my way, I take one in my mouth.

"Fuck, Hudson." The dirtiness in her voice has my dick half hard. One simple graze of her soft fingers against it would have me ready to take her in seconds.

I give the other nipple equal attention, sliding my free hand into the front of her jeans. My fingers tease her swollen bud through the soaked fabric of her panties. I'm hooking the fabric out of the way to touch her wet pussy without any barriers when I hear the creek of the barn door.

I yank my hand out of her jeans and help her fix her shirt as she works at her bra clasp.

"Hudson, you better get back to the rodeo," Natalie calls from the other side of the barn. "You're going to be late,"

"Guess we better go, huh?" Jillian says to me, a wicked smile spread across her swollen lips.

I give her one more quick kiss. "We're not finished."

4

JILLIAN

Sonya's seat in the VIP section is empty when I sit down. The bronc riders are up before the bull riders, so I'm certain she's still hanging out with her cowboy. I'm eager to hear how things went, but relieved to have a few more minutes to myself.

My heart is still racing from that steamy encounter in the barn.

Hudson didn't use any typically cheesy womanizer moves to get me to do what he wanted. I'm still shocked, because what happened in the barn has me all jumbled in the head.

If he didn't live in another state, I would definitely think we were dating now. The way he held my hand on the drive back and put his arm around my back as we walked toward the rodeo area, like he was prepared to protect me should anyone give me a hard time—Darla included no doubt—made it feel like we are...together.

"First time?" Natalie's voice is a surprise, though I should have expected to see her here.

"Yeah, actually."

"I gotta warn you, you'll get hooked."

I'm already hooked on one aspect of the rodeo, no matter the risk. If I get my heart broken after this weekend is over, well, it is what it is now. "I'm okay with that."

"Hudson's a good guy, just so you know." Natalie tilts her full bag of popcorn my way in offering. I scoop up a small handful, happy to have an excuse to keep my mouth busy with anything besides a response. "I know what the media says about him. Even what his brothers think, too. But he's not that guy."

"How do you know?"

"I've known Hudson Wilder since he was five years old. He's always been a social guy. And he has manners that dictate that he be kind to everyone showing him attention. He's got a pure heart. Spend enough time with him, you'll see I'm right and the media has got it all wrong."

The announcer greets the crowd, and soon the cheering makes conversation nearly impossible. Just as well, because I'm suddenly overwhelmed by this new information. I want to believe that Hudson is a good guy, but I thought it was a fantasy playing in my mind. Now, I think it could be reality.

Natalie sits by me as one bronc rider after another enters into the arena. She's kind enough to explain the rules and how the riders score. I'm surprisingly fascinated. Natalie is right. It's easy to get hooked.

Though I'm hardly in a position to pack up my life here and move to Montana, I still hazily daydream about a life with Hudson. Living on a ranch, traveling the country with him on most weekends, celebrating all his victories, and being by his side on those hard nights.

"It's a tough life," Natalie says after the announcer lets the crowd know Hudson Wilder is up next. "Very demanding. And it's hard on the nerves. Every time they ride, they could get hurt. Seriously hurt. To be with a rodeo cowboy is to accept that risk and love them anyway."

When the chute opens and Hudson emerges, my breath paralyzes in my lungs. Despite how fast everything is happening, I can see his smooth, calculated movements. It reminds me of the rocking barrel. I feel closer to him than I thought possible. My nipples tighten, looking forward to finishing what we started.

The buzzer sounds and Hudson jumps off.

"For the record," says Natalie as she stands, "I

love Hudson like a son. I like you, but please don't hurt him."

HUDSON

I'm pulled away for an interview after my ride. Then by a mob of fans wanting autographs and photos. I give everyone the best smile I can, and politely turn down the few offers for my own private after party.

Every minute I'm away from Jillian now that my ride is finished feels like an eternity. Though I have one more night to ride, the ticking clock is against us. I don't want her company for the weekend. I want it for the rest of my life.

Any of my brothers would call me crazy. But I don't care.

Asking someone to live the rodeo circuit life is demanding, but if Jillian really is the one I've been waiting for, she'll be up for the challenge. Hell, with her bold and cunning personality, she'll make it look easy.

I miss Colt's ride by the time I finally make it to the stands to see Jillian. We stay for the remaining riders, but quickly leave when it's over. The four of us—myself, Jillian, Colt, and Jillian's best friend, head into town. I'm the after-party guy who always shows up at whatever bar is hosting. It's good for the local business, and I'm happy to help draw in a crowd. But tonight, I wish I didn't have to be there at all.

"We won't stay long," I say to Jillian.

Colt and *Jane Harper*—I know she's not a writer either, but who am I to spoil their fun?—leave almost right away.

After three or four women try to wedge their way between Jillian and me, I decide I've had enough. Tomorrow I'll be expected to stay a little longer, especially if I win. Which I intend to do. But tonight, I want to ravage the woman latched onto my arm. Make her cry out my name as I claim her as my own. "You ready to get out of here?"

"Please."

We're on the way to the door, shuffling through the crowd, when one of the rodeo girls from earlier slices into our escape path. Jillian is tucked behind me, our fingers laced together.

"You really should reconsider, Hudson." I don't remember her name, but she was definitely the more insistent one from earlier today. I thought I had made it clear to her that I wasn't interested. "Ditch her and come with me. I'll show you a *really* good time."

Before I can say a single word, Jillian darts out around me. "You can move out of the way, sweetheart, or I'll move you myself. Your choice. This cowboy is coming home with *me* tonight."

"Excuse me?"

The last thing I want is a fight to break out between them. I'm firm when I say, "I'm not interested. Have a good night." I tug on Jillian's arm to move her through the bar crowd. I have to admit, that fiery side of hers is quite a turn on.

When we're finally out in the fresh air and the noise of the bar crowd fades away, I pull Jillian into my arms and kiss her greedily. It's a kiss intended to show her exactly how much I want her and no one else.

"Your place or mine?" she asks me in a breathless whisper when our lips finally break apart.

"Well, I'm staying with Natalie…"

"My place it is." We take a couple steps forward before she pulls me to a stop with our connected hands. "But we might piss off my neighbors."

"Looking forward to it."

5

JILLIAN

I'm nervous when the door to my apartment closes. Sonya is spending the night at the hotel with her cowboy, which truly leaves Hudson and me all alone. I've wanted him *bad* since the moment I first laid eyes on him. But it's been a while since I've been with a man.

"You want a beer or glass of water?" I offer, hoping the shakiness in my voice isn't too apparent. Usually I'm bold, but tonight I feel like a fragile little flower. It's the effect Hudson has on me. No one has ever made me feel this way—this vulnerable.

"No thanks."

He clasps my hand in his own and draws me

closer. "Jillian, we don't have to do anything you don't want to."

Oh, but I want to. I want to do *all* the naughty things with him. "I want to, Hudson." To show him I mean it, I slip my shirt over my head and toss it across the room. It lands on a lampshade, causing us both to laugh.

The nervous tension eases and a ravenous hunger takes its place.

Gazes locked, I unclasp my bra and let it drop to the ground. Hudson's dark eyes drench with desire. He closes the distance between us, his hands cupping and squeezing my breasts. I love the feel of his hands on them. The man could bring me to a climax with this alone.

"I really like these," he says before dipping down and teasing my nipples with his teeth.

I palm the front of his jeans, rubbing my hand against his hardening length. He's *huge*. I work at the zipper until it's down then slip my hand inside his pants. Wrapping my hand around his girth, I slowly stroke his cock. A guttural moan escapes him. Fuck it's a sexy sound.

Hudson goes for my neck, nibbling at the sensitive skin. A hand dives into my jeans, searching for my swollen clit. My knees wobble at his touch. "You're so wet, Jilly. So fucking wet." He growls the last words as his fingers push aside my panties. The raw contact of his heated skin against my cunt makes me dizzy.

I shimmy my jeans below my hips to allow him better access. Hudson dips a finger inside me, stroking my nub with his thumb. I cry out his name, not giving a damn if the neighbors pound on the wall before this night is over.

"That's it, babe. Come for me." Hudson quickens his pace, slipping in a second finger. The pressure, the pace, the utter erotic feeling of Hudson pleasuring me in the middle of my living room, still wearing that fucking sexy cowboy hat sends me over the edge.

"Oh. My. God." I can't breathe, and I can barely see straight. Stars. So many stars cloud my vision. My legs topple and I drop onto the couch, jeans still pooled around my ankles.

"That was the hottest thing I've ever seen." He sets his hat on the coffee table and sheds his shirt and jeans before joining me on the couch.

"I—I need a minute. Catching. My. Breath." I've *never* had an orgasm that took me that hard. I hope this is the first of many to come. I kick the jeans off my ankles.

"Of course." Hudson draws me into his arms and kisses my cheek. "But I'm not done with you yet," he growls against my ear. "Just getting started."

My eyes flicker to his massive length pushing against his boxers. I don't know how the hell it's going to fit inside me, but I can't wait to find out. "Bedroom, or?"

"We'll get there, eventually." With another deep, sensual kiss that leaves every nerve ending in my body tingling with desire, Hudson slips my panties off and tosses them away. They join my shirt on the lamp shade.

He stands, and the last piece of clothing separating us—his boxers—drop to the floor. My eyes widen, taking in the full sight of him for the first time. I lick my lips in anticipation of what's to come.

"If you want me to use a condom, I will," Hudson says.

I hesitate. I don't want a thing between us, but what if the media isn't completely wrong?

"I haven't been with a woman in over a year. And never unprotected."

I swallow, the gravity of that confession hitting me. I'd be the first to feel him *completely*.

"We don't need a condom." I spread my legs in invitation and his eyes heat.

I start to turn my body so he can lie down on the couch above me, but he takes my hand and pulls me up instead. "I have a different idea." He leads me to the elevated arm of the couch. "Sit down, right on the edge."

I scoot my bottom as far as I can before it'll fall off the side of the couch. Hudson parts my legs and steps between my legs. "Hold on, babe." He bends his knees, lowering to my center. His hands slide under my thighs to join us together. I arch my back, digging my fingers into the cushion as he enters me.

I gasp.

"You okay, Jilly?"

"More than okay." I thrust my hips toward him, inviting more of his cock in.

"Fuck, you feel perfect."

He fills me completely, and my eyes fall shut. I've never felt so alive or complete in my life. I rock my hips and Hudson starts to rock with me. I feel the scrape of his teeth against a nipple as our pace increases. My legs dangle in the air, unable to touch the ground. I wrap them around his waist, locking them into place with my ankles.

He goes in deeper. Harder.

"Fuck, Hudson." Another orgasm is building, but it's stronger than the first. I'm afraid it's too intense. Too much.

"Look at me, Jilly," says Hudson in the midst of pounding into me. "You're okay. Trust me. Let go of your fears. I've got you. I'll always have you."

"Always?"

"You're mine, Jilly. Only mine now. You got that?"

His words allow me the courage to let go and receive every ounce of pleasure this massive orgasm blasts me with. I shake and cry out his name. The most intense waves of ecstasy I've ever experienced shake me to the damn core. My walls pulse around his cock.

"Did you…"

"Not yet. I'm saving up for the grand finale, babe." He pulls me to my feet, keeping his arms protectively around me as I lead him to my bedroom.

HUDSON

I'll never get enough of Jillian as long as I live. I know that for certain now. It's never felt more right or meant to be with anyone else. She's mine to have, to protect, to hold close. It'll always be this way for me. Whatever our obstacles, we'll figure them out.

"You up for a little reverse cowgirl?" I ask when she opens the door to her bedroom.

"Do I get to ride one-handed?"

I devour her mouth right there in the doorway, my hands smashing against her tits, my cock pressing against her belly. I could fucking take her right here, but the sight of her riding me is too much to pass up.

In a tumble of clumsy steps and hungry groping, we fall onto the bed.

"Roll onto your back, cowboy."

Jillian is on all fours, waiting for me to get situated. Every curvy inch of her is beautiful and so damn sexy. I'm almost too distracted to obey, but I manage to tuck a pillow under my head so I can watch her.

She lifts one leg over me and shimmies her ass until she's positioned right above me. Her soft fingers wrap around my length and stroke it a few times. When she lowers her mouth over my cock, I almost lose it. "Get that sweet pussy in my face. Now."

I lick her wet folds, teasing the very sensitive nub with my tongue as she pleasures my cock. Her deep moans vibrate against my length and nearly send me over the edge. I could come in her mouth, and one day soon I will. But tonight, I need to release myself inside her sweet pussy.

"Stop," I pant.

She gives me a pouty look over her shoulder.

"It feels so fucking good, Jilly. But I want to come inside you."

"Okay, good."

Jillian crawls forward and lowers her pussy onto my cock without much warning. We both cry out. A neighbor pounds on the wall. Neither of us fucking care. She sits back and lifts one hand in the air like she did on the barrel. I thrust into her hard, and she meets my savage pace.

Her blonde waves cascade down her bare back

when she throws her head back and lets out a long moan. I feel her pussy start to clench my dick. I've held back as long as I could. "I'm coming, babe."

I grip her hips as I pump harder, faster. The slapping of our bodies is erotic and raw.

My release knocks into me like a massive wave I didn't see coming. I hold her hips hard against me as my seed fills her. "You're mine now, Jilly. Forever."

6

JILLIAN

I wake up to a flood of texts from my boss. Guess I forgot to hang those for sale signs. And he's *pissed*.

I throw the covers off and fish a new set of clothes out of my dresser while Hudson continues to sleep. My gaze snags on him for a moment, and every thing we did last night replays in my mind. A wicked smile forms on my lips.

But I only get a few seconds to enjoy the sight of a hot cowboy in my bed because my phone buzzes again.

I punch out a text to tell my boss something came up yesterday, promising to get all the signs up this morning. I ignore his response. It's not likely to be very kind. Some irritated seller probably interrupted his morning romp.

Sometimes, I really wish I could tell him to take this job and shove it. Being his personal assistant has been one of the least exciting things of my adult life. My eyes drop onto Hudson's naked body, only partially hidden by the sheet. I bet he's ten years older than me. He's lived a lot of life—an *exciting* life. The whole idea is thrilling.

Would it be so crazy to ditch this life for one with him?

But Natalie's words repeat in my mind. *It's a tough life. Very demanding. And hard on the nerves.*

As exciting and sexy as it is to me that Hudson is a bronc rider, it's dangerous. Natalie didn't spare me any details when she told me about a ride gone bad three or four years ago. Hudson broke his leg in three different places. In one spot, the bone had been shattered.

Riders put themselves at serious risk.

There'd be highs and lows.

The urge to leave and hang those signs is overwhelming. I need some space to think, to clear my head. Hudson told me last night that I was his. *Forever*. I've heard players use those same words, but Hudson meant them. The sincerity of what he said to me still makes my heart swell.

But if we're going to make this work...I just need

time to make sure it's what I want. It's all happening so fast.

I leave a note on the nightstand to let him know I have to work this morning. I don't want to alarm him about needing space, so I don't mention it. I fight the urge to kiss him so I don't wake him. We were up quite late last night, and I know he needs his rest for the last night of the rodeo.

But mostly, I need to sneak out without waking him so I can figure all this out.

HUDSON

I stretch lazily in the comfortable bed, but my hands don't find Jillian where I left her. I'm exhausted from our late night, but I don't regret a second of it. I have plenty of time to rest up and get my head on straight before tonight. My dick begins to harden again, and I'm hoping she's up for another round.

Naked, I stroll into the apartment hoping to find her in the kitchen or in the shower. There's plenty I could do to her in the shower.

"Jilly?" I call out. "Are you home?"

I return to the bedroom and find a note on the nightstand.

Have to work this morning. Boss is super pissed. Pot

of coffee in the kitchen. Please lock the door behind you. See you tonight. XOXO

I frown at the note, reading it three or four times. Why didn't she wake me up? I don't even know what it is she does for a living, but she never mentioned having to work on Saturday morning. The mention of her boss is what throws me. Did she get called in?

Doubt begins to fill me as I gather my clothes strewn across her living room. I don't know what ties Jilly has to this city. I don't know what I'd be asking her to leave behind. My brothers and I have a ranch, and there's nothing in this world that could make me walk away from it. It's been in our family for generations. So me moving here is out of the question.

I can picture Jillian living with me on that ranch though, on our own private corner. Raising a family there together. But could she be happy in Montana, giving up her life, friends, and maybe even family here?

Skipping the coffee, I get dressed and head back to the rodeo grounds to find my brothers. I know Colt will need someone to talk to, and I'm hoping Austin might be up for letting me chew his ear off.

I don't know what I'm going to do about Jillian. I love her. I just hope we can figure out a future together.

7

JILLIAN

I'm shaky when I arrive at the rodeo grounds. I'm about to make the biggest decision of my life tonight—about to put myself out there in a way I never have before. But spending the day without Hudson has made me realize just how much I want to be with him.

Halfway to the gate behind the VIP stands, I'm cut off by the skinny rodeo girl from the bar last night. I'm incredibly low on patience right now. "What do you want?" I snap.

"I hope you enjoyed last night," she says to me with an air of confidence that is sickening. She reminds me of one of the mean girls in high school who used to call me chubby. I only put up with that for a *very* short period of time before I put that girl in her place. I can put this one in hers too.

"I enjoyed it in ways you can't even pretend to fantasize, honey."

Surprise flashes in her eyes, but it's gone quickly. "Well, tonight, Hudson Wilder is going home with me."

I laugh in her face, loudly and obnoxiously. Not even to be mean. It's because her prissy self is *so* convinced she has any hold over Hudson. "Good luck with that."

Her mouth is agape when I shove my way around her and head toward the section behind the stands. I'm not even sure if they'll let me in, but I'll think of something. I'm good at that. I know in the depths of my soul that Hudson is not the player the media would like everyone to think he is. I have no doubts at all that he's exactly the man he claims to be.

"Who you with, darling?" An older gentleman at the gate asks me.

"Hudson Wilder." I have no way to prove it without the man going to Hudson and asking him. Considering I left the cowboy alone in my apartment with nothing but a note this morning, I'm not sure how excited he'll be to see me. So maybe claiming to be his girlfriend—which we haven't exactly nailed down anyway—might be a poor tactic.

"Hudson you say?"

"He promised me a quick interview." I might look more convincing with a notepad or something, but I'm winging it here. "For my next book."

I see Darla out of the corner of my eye, leading the gaggle of actual romance authors to the VIP stands. She catches a glimpse of me, and her eyes narrow. I turn my back, praying she doesn't blow my cover.

"He doesn't have long before the draw, you know."

"I promise I won't keep him long."

Just as Darla starts to march my way, the gentleman opens the gate and lets me through. "He'll be down by that tent with the blue tarp most likely."

"Thank you, kind sir." I pat the older man on the shoulder, earning a smile in return. Two steps away, I start to run. I'm afraid Darla is about to rat me out.

I'm panting by the time I reach the open blue-tarped tent. Running is among my least favorite things. But I have to find Hudson before I lose my nerve. I scan the tent, finding a table of food. Several pairs of eyes look up at me from around that table. I don't recognize anyone, but a couple of them could be the brothers he mentioned.

"Can we help you?" one asks.

"I'm looking for Hudson."

Understanding settles in his expression. "You're Jillian."

"Yep, guilty." I nervously look over my shoulder, not surprised to see Darla trotting toward me with vengeance in her eyes. Who knew crashing a tiny private event would cause a woman such fury? "Is he around?"

"I'm Austin, one of his brothers."

"The pickup man?"

"That's the one." Austin holds out his arm in invitation. "C'mon, I'll take you to him."

I've just looped my arm through Austin's when I hear Darla's sharp, nasally tone. "Stop right there!"

"I swear this woman needs to get laid or something," I mutter under my breath. But apparently it was loud enough for Austin to hear, because he lets out a chuckle.

"What do you want?" I ask Darla, exasperated.

"You're not a *real* author. There is no Mandi Flowers."

Austin quirks an eyebrow at me in curiosity. "Long story," I tell him. I'm just about to tell Darla off—because seriously, I've had enough of people pushing me around today—when Hudson appears at my side.

"Jilly?"

"Hey."

Darla's reprimanding me for false identity or some such thing. But I don't care what she's saying.

All that matters is what I need to confess to Hudson. I turn to him, completely blocking out the irritated woman behind me. A quick glance around tells me she's annoying most everyone.

"I'll get rid of her," Austin says with a tip of his hat.

"What are you doing back here?" Hudson asks, shoving his hands into his front pockets. He's as nervous as I am. It should help me relax, but those damn butterflies in my stomach are throwing a rave.

"I came to see you."

"Did you now?"

"I'm sorry I left this morning. I really *did* have to work. But that won't come up again."

"No?"

"I quit my job."

"What?"

"I was working for some womanizing asshole. It paid the bills, but I've been miserable. I don't want to work a job just to pay bills if it means being treated like dirt. What kind of life is that?"

His hands slide out of his pockets and gently cup my arms. The heat of his touch scorches my skin, and I hope he never lets go. "What are you saying, Jilly?"

"I know this is crazy, but I'm crazy sometimes. And I'm just going to put it all out there. I love you, Hudson Wilder. I don't want this weekend to be all that we have. I want more. I want it all."

His smile illuminates his entire face and his eyes sparkle with happiness. "You would give this all up for me?" He waves his hand around, obviously indicating the city life.

"Yes." My family might not approve of my rash decision, but I know my bestie will understand. "I've never worked a day on a ranch before. But I'm a fast learner."

"The rodeo life is a hard life, Jilly."

"I know. I'm up for the challenge."

"You're sure about this?"

"Completely."

He draws me into his arms, brushing away the windblown hair from my cheek. "I want it all, too, Jilly. I love you. And if you'll move to Montana to be with me, I'll love you every day of your life. *Our* life."

Snaking my hands behind his neck, I draw him down for a kiss hot enough to burn any of the pages those *real* romance authors have written. "Better get to the draw, cowboy."

"You'll be here?"

"Always."

EPILOGUE

HUDSON

It's been four wonderful years with Jillian, and I will never get enough of this woman and the family we've created. "You ready?" I ask Jilly, taking her hand. Parker, our three-year-old, is hanging out on my shoulders. That kid has the rodeo spark in his eyes.

"What are you up to, Hudson?" She squeezes my hand with hers, and rubs her round belly with the other. Soon, we'll have a new member of the Wilder clan.

I lead her to the barn, and I still don't think she suspects a thing.

"I'm not getting on that barrel," she says in her firmest tone. "Not six months pregnant."

I let out an easy laugh at that. Of course Jillian would think that's what I'm up to. I love how this woman still makes me laugh so often just by being herself. It's the most refreshing part of any day. "I promise, it's not that."

"I'd ask for a hint, but you're not really a fan of those."

At the barn door, I set Parker down. "You don't need a hint. We're here." I open the door and let her go inside first.

We're early, but I wanted this time with my family before the rest of the Wilders bombard the occasion. I follow my wife and son inside, poking at a low-hanging balloon on my way in.

Jilly's eyes fixate on the banner pinned up on the back wall. "Retirement party?" she reads, a question in her voice. She spins toward me. "Hudson, what is this about?"

I take her hands in mine. Parker wraps himself around her leg, but is quickly distracted by the floating balloons and skitters off after one. "This is about our family."

"*You're* retiring?"

"Yes." It's the middle of the season, and I'm ranking well. But I'm tired of traveling. Tired of leaving my family behind on the weekends I'm gone and they can't go with me. "I'm ready to be home. With my family." I nod at Parker. "I'm ready to train the next generation."

Jilly's hands reach up to my cheeks and draw me down for a kiss. It quickly turns hungry. If Parker weren't in the barn with us, I'd be about to do some very dirty things to my wife right now. "Tonight, you're all mine."

"Promise?"

"Always."

AUSTIN

WILDER BROTHERS RODEO BOOK 3

1

LIZ

"What do you mean you signed me up?" I ask my sister, Gemma. I try to keep my voice low considering we're in the stands at the local rodeo and there are people everywhere. Some of them know me, too. I don't need any comments from the peanut gallery about my dating life.

"Exactly what it sounds like." A mischievous twinkle dances in her eyes. "You've got a chance to go on a date with the hunky Austin Wilder."

I shake my head violently *no*. I don't do blind dates—I don't even do *dates* anymore. After the pitiful luck I've had, I'm determined they're a waste of time. Last week's tragic date solidified my resolve.

No more. I'm better off single and focused on my own goals. My bakery isn't going to open itself.

The anticipation of a date involves too much excitement, prep, and nerves only to be let down by yet another dud or douchecanoe. It's all wasted time that could be spent on finalizing my business plan or testing out a new recipe.

"Un-sign me up."

Gemma shrugs nonchalantly, glancing around at the gathering crowd as we wait for the event to start. "Sorry, too late for that."

I clench the program in my fist, crumbling the side. *Austin Wilder: Pickup Man* jumps out at me in big bold letters above my thumb. Just what I need. A possible blind date with an arrogant cowboy. Seriously, I should write a book about my disastrous dating history. I could sell copies in my future bakery. Gemma might sue me for slander, though, considering she's responsible for over half of them and I *would* let the world know.

"If I win, I'm never going to forgive you." My sister is *always* meddling in my non-existent love life. I know she means well, but it never bodes well for me. I'm the one who has to be the bad guy when it doesn't work out.

"Relax, Liz. You're just one name in dozens. Maybe hundreds. The odds of *you* winning a blind date with Austin are slim."

Letting out an annoyed sigh, I finally take the

time to skim the advertisement in the program. The Wilder brothers are local legends around these parts; the closest thing our town has to celebrities. The four of them all are heavily involved in the rodeo. They travel together, work together, and even own a ranch outside of town together. Plus, they're all smoking hot.

The oldest two are married with families now, but the youngest two are single. And apparently Austin Wilder has decided to offer himself up as a prize tonight.

His pixelated black and white photo sucks me into a trance. There's something about those dark eyes and his half smile. It promises he's up to no good. Against my better judgement, my nipples tighten and pebble. *Ugh!*

Now look, I think a cowboy is just as sexy as the next girl. Add to that he's a *rodeo* cowboy, and well, it's enough to set any sensible girl's panties aflame. But the popularity this man has amassed has obviously gone to his head. Presenting himself up as some sort of grand prize... *puh-leeze!*

"If I win, I'm declining," I declare, panties be damned.

Gemma tosses popcorn at me, and it bounces off my nose into my nacho cheese. I eat it anyway, maintaining eye contact, just to annoy her. "Yeah right," she scoffs. "You're not going to shut him down in front of a crowd."

"Watch me." But the words are a bluff. I have to live in this town, and don't need to be shunned by the masses for embarrassing a local celebrity. "These are all what if's anyway," I counter. "You said it yourself. I'm up against probably a hundred other names in that hat. No way they draw mine." I feel myself start to relax into my own words of wisdom, despite the nagging whisper in the back of my mind trying to sabotage my peace.

"What's your deal with Austin Wilder anyway?" Gemma asks. "Have you met the guy before or something?"

"Yes." Not a lie. I *did* meet him once, in a gas station. The Wilder brothers don't come into town much. They're gone a lot, and when they're home, rumor is they like to enjoy their peace and quiet on their ranch.

Well, *meet* is a strong word. I was standing three people back behind him in line. He didn't even see me. That was months ago. I try to conjure the memory, certain he exuded some form of arrogance or cockiness that'll prove my case. But I come up blank. "Look, I'm done dating for a while. I'm tired. Really tired. Especially after last week."

"I'm sorry," says Gemma with a cringe. Last week was her fault and she can't deny it. "I know I've set you up on some ... less than ideal dates, but—"

I laugh so hard I snort soda out my nose. Which also makes Gemma laugh. "Gemma, you set me up with a personal trainer who couldn't stop talking about protein shakes and supplements." Never mind that I hate the gym and love my curves, thank you very much, but this guy was something else.

"He wasn't *that* bad."

I narrow my eyes at her. "He showed up to our date with a six-week personal training program and meal plan with my name on it."

"Okay, okay. So that one was a mistake."

I wave the flyer, still clenched tight in my grip, at her. "This one is too. You just better hope they don't draw my name."

AUSTIN

"Who's ready for some bull riding action?" The announcer, Ted, calls to the crowd. I'm sitting on my horse in the arena, ready to save any bull rider from certain death should one of the beasts decide to show his temper tonight. That's my job. To stay on my horse, watch the rider and the bull's every move, and pick up the rider once he falls or jumps off his bull should he find himself the beast's target.

Though the job I've had for years always gets my heart pumping, it's pounding now for an entirely different reason.

When the crowd calms, Ted continues. "Before we introduce our bull riders, let's do a last call for our special event of the night—winning a date with the pickup man, Austin Wilder."

I swallow, already regretting my decision. But I lift my hat from my head and wave it toward the crowd like I'm excited.

I did it to help out a friend. The rodeo in my hometown is the most special venue to me out of all the places I've traveled in the country. It's where my brothers and I all got our start. A couple of weeks ago, the owner confessed to me that he's been having troubles this season filling the stands and staying in the black.

To help alleviate his worries, I offered to do something crazy.

I gave up myself as a raffle prize.

"All you single ladies out there," Ted calls out to the crowd. "If you haven't signed up for your chance to win a date with Austin Wilder, you still have time. We'll be drawing the winner halfway through the bull riders. Grab your tickets before it's too late. Grab as many as you want."

Yep. I'm giving myself up as some stranger's date. Tomorrow. Even agreed to take her back to my ranch for a quiet picnic away from the gossipy hens in town. If I'm not careful, one of them would have me married off by sundown. I really hope I don't regret this.

Though I certainly know a few rodeo cowboys who are a little full of themselves, that's not me at all. And had my older brother Hudson not been married with a family, I would've suggested him in a heartbeat. He always did have a suave way with events like these.

But out of the four of us brothers, Tex was the only other option besides myself. And Tex has sworn off women. After what his ex pulled, I can't say I blame the man.

On cue, I take a lap around the edge of the arena to wave at the crowd and let them get a more up close and personal view of me, hoping it'll sell a few more tickets. All the proceeds are going straight to the venue to help catch it up and stay in the black.

I lift my hat and wave it to the crowd again.

That's when I catch a glimpse of the beauty in the stands. Her deep green eyes meet mine and I swear the woman can see clear into my soul.

I send her a smile. She returns it with a scowl and a roll of her eyes.

"Ladies, who out there has bought a ticket or ten?" Ted asks as I turn around and ride by again. It wasn't part of the original plan, but I want a second look at the mystery woman who's captured my interest.

Dozens of hands fly up. But hers doesn't.

I frown for a moment, but replace it with a smile. Part of the rodeo involves putting on a show for the crowd. That's one of the reasons they keep coming back.

"Would you look at that, Austin?" Ted cackles over the loudspeaker. "Who knew this town had so many single ladies?"

Because I can't help myself, I give the mystery beauty a wink before I ride back to the other side of the arena. The sight of her eyes widening in surprise makes my evening. I might have to spend tomorrow with some woman I can't stand fawning all over me. But I *will* find out who my girl is before the night is over if it's the last thing I do.

2

LIZ

"He winked at you!" Gemma clutches my arm in a near death-grip as she squeals in delight. Luckily, the dull roar of the crowd muffles her to most of the people around us. But more eyes than I'd like turn in my direction.

"He did not."

"Did too."

I clamp my lips shut in annoyance, because yes, my sister is right. The showboat did wink at me. That was after he smiled at me and I rolled my eyes in return. He might have everyone else in the audience fooled, but not me. At least that's what I tell myself. "He was showing off," I finally say.

"Liz, that's his job. To *entertain* the crowd."

I wave the flyer at her again. I've read his bio a couple of times now, afraid what my sister may have gotten me into. I know it's a long shot to win, but I tend to win the things I don't want. That's why I have a gnarly feeling about this raffle. "There's a guy for entertaining. See, he's standing in the middle on top of that cage thing. Austin's job is to save guys if a bull charges after them."

"You sure know a lot about this guy for all your talk about not wanting to go on a date with him."

Gemma has always had an uncanny ability to rile me up for her own amusement. I don't take the bait. "You're getting ahead of yourself. They haven't drawn the winner yet."

"Honey, I don't think it matters if you win or not." Gemma nods toward Austin. Even with the man on the opposite side of the arena and his cowboy hat shading his face, he's definitely looking my way.

Tingles skitter throughout my body. I hate to admit that those dark eyes have power over me, even from a distance. I feel exposed and vulnerable, and a wicked part of me likes it.

"Why didn't *you* put your name in the hat?" I ask, hoping to deflect some attention. For as much as Gemma likes to try to set me up with this date or that, she seems to keep her own dating schedule very open. She claims she's picky. But I think there's something she's not telling me. "Or did you buy a raffle ticket, too?"

"No," Gemma admits, fiddling with her nearly empty bag of popcorn. "Austin's not my type."

I follow her flittering gaze to the man in the center of the ring: Tex Wilder. He's got on a ridiculous outfit and a bit of makeup, but anyone with a Facebook account that follows the Wilder brothers knows that he's incredibly attractive under that getup. "Ah, I see."

"Look." Gemma whaps me on the arm with the back of her hand and points to the center of the arena where a line of cowboys march out in a single line. "They're starting."

So my sister has a crush on Tex. *Interesting.* I want to press her for more, ask her if that's why she's turned down other men. But I feel the intense gaze falling on me from across the arena. Austin seems fixated on me. I want to brush it off as my overactive imagination, but I can't shake it.

"I need more nachos," I tell Gemma.

She shackles my wrist and yanks me back to my seat. "Sit."

With introductions finished, the first rider prepares to compete. The chute opens and the clock starts. The audience focuses on the rider and the bull. But my traitorous eyes keep landing on Austin.

He's intensely fixated on the rider, shuffling his

horse to ensure he's always right where he needs to be should the rider require saving, but never in the way.

"Ah, so close," says Gemma.

I didn't even notice that the rider didn't make eight seconds. I was too enamored with Austin and his unyielding focus. It's ... *sexy*.

Ride after ride, I'm consumed with Austin Wilder's ability to work his magic. The first time he has to grab a rider and gallop off to safety from an angry bull, my heart leaps into my throat. The rider climbs the fence and hops over, and Austin is forced to run his horse around the ring until the bull finally loses interest and leaves willingly.

My heart pounds in my ears from the adrenaline rush.

"You like him, don't you?" Gemma asks.

"What?" I shake my head. "No. I'm just watching the show."

"Ladies and gentleman," the announcer says to the crowd. "We're taking a short intermission before the next flight. Let's find out who our lucky lady is. Which one of you will win a private date for two with Austin Wilder?"

Reality returns, and every bad date I've been on in the last month flashes through my mind like a bad trip. But dammit, there's a small part of me—somewhere in the region tingling between my legs—that *wants* to win.

"Fingers crossed!" Gemma squeals.

"What? No! Uncross them."

"I may have bought you more than one ticket."

"And the winner is—"

"Gemma! What did you do? How many?"

"A few ... dozen."

"Liz Hollingsworth."

AUSTIN

The woman sitting beside my mystery beauty squeals with excitement, clapping her hands together. *Liz Hollingsworth.* I'd be lying if I said I wasn't disappointed. I wish it was the woman sitting beside her in the green blouse that matches her intimidatingly beautiful eyes. They might even be sisters from their resemblance.

I nod my head toward the stands, forcing a smile I don't feel to acknowledge the winner.

Well, this just got awkward.

"No, not me," I hear a woman's voice over the clapping. "She's Liz."

My eyes snap up. The woman I thought won is pointing to the one beside her. My breath hitches in my lungs. I was certain by that scowl earlier that she didn't buy a ticket, yet somehow she won. Maybe she bought one for the sake of charity.

I ride across the arena and stop when I'm as close to her as I can get without dismounting and tip my hat. "Ms. Hollingsworth." At least a dozen women around her ooh and ahh in that romantic way. Normally it would drive me nuts, but right now I find it fitting. "Will you join me for a date tomorrow?"

The crowd stills as one of the announcing crew holds a microphone out to her. She notices that her face is now front and center on the big screen and a smile finally stretches across those pretty lips. But something wilder dances in those eyes.

For a split second, I fear she's about to turn me down. My heart thrums erratically in my chest. And it has nothing to do with the possibility of being embarrassed in front of all these people. Only that she might deny me the one thing I'm craving most: the pleasure of her company. I've been drawn to her since the first moment I saw her.

The next rider is preparing to mount his bull. This announcement wasn't supposed to drag out. So I do what I do best in situations like this. I improvise with humor. "Unless horseback riding and romantic picnic dinners at sunset aren't your thing?"

The crowd erupts in a collective, easy laugh. And for the first time I see a genuine smile from Liz. "Yes, I'll go on a date with you."

It takes a lot of effort to hide my relief from the big screen, but I manage. "I look forward to it." Because I know it'll rile up the crowd in a good way and leave her a little annoyed, I give her a wink before I ride off and resume my place.

3

LIZ

"You're not wearing that," Gemma says disapprovingly from my bedroom doorway.

"Why not?" I turn in the mirror, content with my black leggings and light pink cotton shirt. My outfit is comfortable and casual. Exactly the message I want to send since I don't need Austin getting the wrong idea. I may have won a date with the cowboy, but I still stand by my resolve. I have a bakery to focus on, and once our date today is over, that will be my one and only priority.

Gemma marches into my room and straight for my closet. Before I know what's happening, clothes are flying onto my bed by the dozens. "I hope this is not how you've been dressing for all your other dates."

"So what if it is?" It's a total lie, but I can't deny my opportunity to rile *her* up this time.

"You can't be serious."

"Relax, Gem."

She tosses a pair of skinny jeans onto my pillow like they're special and dives back into my closet. I stare at them grudgingly. I don't put on jeans for just anyone. I'd sooner wear a dress, but I don't think it'd go well with horseback riding.

"He *likes* you, Liz." She emerges with a floral print blouse that falls off at the shoulders, setting it next to the jeans. "Give the man a fighting chance."

I shimmy out of my super comfy leggings and into the dreaded jeans of torture. The *only* plus is that they do make my legs look super sexy. "He doesn't even know me. It'll take minutes for him to realize we have nothing in common. I've never even ridden a horse. And look at me, Gem. I'm not some skinny rodeo girl in Daisy Dukes, and I have no desire to be."

"You're beautiful, Liz. Stunning even. You wear confidence like a second skin, so go out on this date and own that. Plus, it's even *more* romantic that he gets to teach you how to ride a horse. Seriously, do you even watch chick flicks anymore?"

Our gaze locks across my bed, now filled with

way too many clothes. I hope Gemma plans to hang all the rejects back up while I'm out.

It's been eons since we feasted on popcorn and M&Ms and watched a rom com together. "It's probably those movies that turned you into my personal matchmaker," I retort with a playful smile.

"You can't prove it." Gemma hands me the floral blouse. "Put this on. It's perfect for a date with a cowboy."

"Yes, boss."

Once I'm dressed, Gemma studies me far too closely. "Turn."

I obey because it's easier than arguing. My ride will be here in ten minutes, and I'm suddenly more eager to leave than to stay. Who knows what Gemma would come up with if she had too much time to work with.

After several minutes, my makeup is applied to perfection and Gemma's worked magic with a flatiron I can never seem to figure out. She's just unleashing a can of hairspray when I hear the doorbell.

"He's here!" Gemma squeals. She manages to release a light layer of spray before I rush out of the room choking on a small cloud. I slip into a pair of cowgirl boots she let me borrow and grab a light denim jacket for when the sun goes down.

Austin Wilder stands on the other side of the screen door, glancing away over his shoulder. It gives me an excuse to take all of him in. Damn, I can't deny that he's attractive. The sexy way he looks in those Wranglers should be outlawed. My tightening nipples can attest.

He turns his head and our eyes meet. His smile makes my heart pitter-patter in my chest. I feel like a shy teenager going on her first date with a boy she really likes. It's ... odd. "Hey," Austin says from the other side of the door. "You look amazing, Liz."

"Th—thanks."

Gemma comes up behind me and opens the door, inviting him inside like I seem to have forgotten how to do. "Hey Austin! I'm Liz's sister, Gemma."

"Nice to meet you."

"She's the reason you're stuck with me tonight." It's a sad attempt at humor to ease my frayed nerves. I should *not* be so nervous about a date I never even wanted.

"It's true. I bought her fifty tickets."

My eyes widen to twice their normal size. "*Fifty?*" She's been pushy about dates before, but even for Gemma, that's excessive.

"You two have fun!" Gemma shoves me closer to Austin because my feet have apparently forgotten how to function on their own. Against my ear she whispers, "If you don't come home tonight, that's okay."

AUSTIN

Years of rodeo life in front of crowds have taught me how to appear cool and collected even when I'm rattled with nerves. The woman I spotted in the stands last night was gorgeous, but now that I get to see her up close, I'm paralyzed by her stunning beauty. Her wavy auburn curls cascade down her shoulders, brushing her tits. I shouldn't look, but I can't help it. I spent most of last night dreaming of her naked. And don't get me started on those jeans and the way they accentuate her curves.

"Ready?" It's the only word I can choke out. I feel like a giddy teenage boy who won the lottery.

She nods, flashing me a simple smile. Maybe she's just as nervous as I am.

Her sister shoves Liz the rest of the way out the door. "Have fun you two!"

I lead her to the truck, adjusting the front of my jeans as discreetly as I can. My lusty dreams seem to be on replay now that she's in my presence. I'm drawn to Liz in a way I've never been drawn to a woman before, and it's not just that floral scent luring me in. It's more. So much more.

"Let me help you up," I tell her after opening the truck door, offering my hand. It's all I can do to keep it from straying. I want to run my fingers along her curves, with or without clothes. Right now, I just want to touch her.

"Thank you," she says to me once seated. Liz reaches for her seatbelt, but I step up and take it from her.

"Allow me."

I buckle her in, and damned if the backs of my fingers don't graze one of her tits. Her quiet gasp doesn't escape me, but when I meet her eyes to apologize, I see desire lingering. "I've never ridden a horse before." Her words are quick and breathy, but they put me at ease.

"I'll teach you." I tuck a stray wavy lock behind her ear. "I'll keep you safe, don't you worry." I want to kiss her, right there in the driveway with her sister peeking from behind the curtain. Liz wets her lips.

"I hate pancakes," Liz blurts.

For a second, I'm stunned into confused silence. But quickly, laughter builds inside until I can't hold it in. "Good, me too." The tension from a moment ago dissipates slightly, allowing me to hop out of the truck like the gentleman I'm trying to be.

"I don't know why I said that," says Liz. "I never say things like that."

I chuckle, still amused. It makes me feel in control again to know that I make her a little nervous. Especially after the scowl she was so quick to give me last night. Any fears I had of her being miserable during our date are disappearing. "I don't like grits, breakfast sausage, or waffles, while we're on the topic. But I'd eat the crap out of a fresh, gooey cinnamon roll all day long."

"I make the best cinnamon rolls." A smile eases onto her lips, and she might even be flirting a little with me.

Unable to resist, I reach across the center console for her hand. Electricity rushes through my entire body at the contact. It's all I can do to focus on driving. "You might have to prove that to me."

"I'm opening a bakery," she says with the utmost confidence. "Breakfast pastries are a specialty of mine."

Yep, I'm screwed. I know I just met Liz, but I know deep in my soul she's mine. I'm going to spend the day showing her exactly what I'm feeling.

4

LIZ

I've had the most amazing day with Austin. He taught me how to ride a horse, and then we rode along the trails on his family ranch. I've always lived in town where things never stop moving, but the quiet is enticing. I can see why he loves it out here so much.

"Ready for our picnic?" he asks as we slow the horses.

I've been at ease since we started riding—though I will admit my rear end is a little sore. Ignoring the undercurrent of sexual tension has been easier to manage with space between us. But now that we're about to be close on a blanket with a magnificent view of the mountains in the distance, I'm nervous again.

This is ridiculous, as I've tried to remind myself time and time again. I'm not dating Austin—I'm not dating *anyone*. Not interested in dating. I'm focusing on opening my bakery. And there are still tons of tasks to complete before that is even a possibility. I let my gaze linger on Austin. Falling for a man like him ... I'd fall fast and hard. It'd be explosive, consuming, and dangerous. I'm afraid to lose myself.

Swinging my leg over the side of the horse to dismount, I realize my other foot is not planted in the stirrup like I thought. I let out a tiny scream and wait to slam into the ground, certain my graceful ways with a horse will keep Austin uninterested.

But strong arms catch me inches before I hit the dirt.

"You okay?" Austin asks, concern in his eyes, as he lifts me to my feet. The security I feel in his arms is intoxicating.

"Yep. Yep, I'm good." I wiggle my way out of his arms before I do something I can't come back from. Like pull his lips down to mine and kiss him until he's stolen all my oxygen. I take a couple steps back and stroke my horse's neck. "Thanks."

He tips his hat in response. "Let me get everything set up."

I can't seem to keep my feet to stay still as Austin spreads out a blanket and unpacks a picnic basket.

I'm too antsy to join him, because all I can think about is shoving the food aside and using that blanket for other things—like rolling around on it naked with a cowboy.

Wow, this escalated quickly.

"Come, sit down." Austin waits for me to move forward, refusing to take his own seat until I take one first. When I hesitate too long, he asks, "Do I make you uncomfortable, Liz? We can go back if you want."

"No. Nope. Not at all. It's just—well, see. I'm doing this not-dating thing. Gemma—this is all her fault you should know—put my name in the hat *fifty* times." I can't seem to stop myself from rambling like a complete idiot as Austin takes slow steps toward me. "I just want to focus on my bakery and—well, not date. It's been such a disaster lately, and I don't have the time." Austin removes his hat and tosses it onto the blanket. He's close enough for me to reach out and touch, but my mouth won't stop. "Did I mention I might write a book about—"

Lips swoop down and capture mine, and *finally* I shut up. My entire world spins in fast, dizzying circles. I've spent hours with this man pretending like we're just friends, but now that we're off the horses and in each other's arms, it's impossible to deny. I want him.

"Better?" he asks, his lips just a breath away.

"Much." Though I'm not sure my legs will function once he lets go.

"My aunt fixed us a tasty lunch. I promise you'll love it." Austin puts his arm around my back and leads me to the blanket. My steps are wobbly but I make it without faceplanting. It's the little things.

When Austin lets go, all I feel is his absence. I don't like it one bit. I've had my crushes, and dated a couple of guys I liked. But I've never been this intensely drawn to anyone. And that was *before* the earthshattering kiss. I think I'm in a lot of trouble.

AUSTIN

Watching Liz bite into a strawberry is officially the sexiest thing I've ever witnessed. I hadn't planned to kiss her earlier—I was going to wait until the end of the date like a true gentleman. But dammit, she was so adorable rambling on and on. I *had* to kiss her.

Now that I've tasted her sweet lips, I need to taste them again.

"Tell me more about your bakery," I say, refilling her glass with wine and hoping she doesn't notice my hands shaking as I hand it over.

"It's just a business plan right now." The sparkle in her eyes tells me this is a very big dream of hers.

"But I've always wanted to open a bakery in my mom's name. She's the one who taught me to bake, and I want to share her recipes. I promise you, her cinnamon rolls are like an orgasm in your mouth." Liz swats her hand over her mouth, her eyes widening in shock.

I let out an unguarded laugh. She's so damn cute when she's embarrassed.

"I can't believe I just said that." She looks down at her glass. "I blame the wine."

Reaching my hand toward her chin, I trace her wine-stained lips with my finger. "An orgasm in your mouth, huh? I'd sure like to experience that."

The air between us has been charged since I arrived at her house, but now it's an electrical storm of desire. It's taking all my restraint not to climb on top of her and ravage her on this blanket. My eyes drop to the dip in her blouse, longing for her tits in my mouth.

Instead, I kiss the hollow spot along her neck. Her hand fists in my hair as she lets out the softest moan.

I take her wine glass from her, helping myself to a hearty sip to calm my nerves. I'm never nervous around a woman, but I sure as hell am around Liz. I set it on the picnic basket so it doesn't spill.

"If you want me to stop, you have to tell me Liz." I slide my hand beneath the hem of her flowery shirt, giving her time to tell me to quit before things progress. My fingers graze the lace of her bra, causing my dick to harden beneath my zipper. Our mouths fuse together as my hand cups her tit and squeezes. She moans into my mouth and pulls me closer.

Lifting her blouse, I expose her bra. I know there's a ravenous look in my eyes as I feast on the sight of her tits in that sexy fabric. "Blue lace. My favorite." I dip my fingers into the top of her bra until her hard nipple is free and pinch it between my fingers gently.

"Austin," she says my name in a breathless pant.

I take her nipple into my mouth and suckle it, earning more sexy moans. She leans back on her hands, giving me better access to her tits. I unsnap her bra clasp, freeing the magnificent wonders. As I take the opposite nipple into my mouth to pleasure, I ease my hand into the waist of her jeans.

"Austin, I—"

Inches from her pussy, I stop sliding my hand beneath her jeans. It's one of the greatest tortures I've ever known. "If you want me to stop, Liz, tell me."

"I—I can't promise anything—"

"You don't have to." I don't want Liz to feel an ounce of pressure. We're meant to be together, and I know she'll come to realize it sooner or later. But I won't demand it of her. If this is real between us, she'll figure it out for herself. "Let me pleasure you, sweetheart. I'll make you see the stars before they come out tonight."

Her deep green eyes are drenched with want. "Okay."

I kiss her deeply, with a hunger consuming the both of us. Undoing the button of her jeans, I slide my hand home to her wet center. Right now, the only thing I care about is Liz's pleasure. I don't have to worry about the future, because I know the orgasm I'm about to give her will leave her begging for more. And when she does, I'll claim her as my own.

My lips capture one nipple, one hand massages the opposite tit, and the other dives beneath her panties until it finds her swollen clit. I flicker it slowly at first. But as I switch my mouth to the other nipple, I increase my pace.

"Austin," Liz cries out, her fingers digging into my shoulder. "Oh my god, Austin!"

I work my hand as quickly as it'll go. She rocks her hips to meet my rhythm. "That's it, sweetheart. I want to show you the stars. Come for me."

She cries out long and loud as she shudders against my hand. Fuck me, it's hot.

5

LIZ

Austin's right.

I'm seeing stars. So many stars.

"Wow," I gasp, barely able to form words because I'm still panting so hard from that climax. I've had orgasms before, but never one like *that*.

"That's just a preview, sweetheart." Austin kisses me softly on the lips as he shimmy's his hand out of my jeans. When he pulls back, he licks my juices from his fingers. "Sweet. Just like I knew you would taste."

I'm incredibly turned on. What would it be like to have Austin's mouth on my pussy? The very thought makes my entire body heat, despite its current recovery from that first, powerful orgasm.

I want more. So much more.

The thought thrills and terrifies me. I'm still determined to stick to my resolve, now more than ever. If I give into Austin, I know that'll be it. I'll be so consumed with my desire for him that I might lose my focus on the bakery. He's *that* dangerous.

Yet, all I can think about is unbuckling his jeans and lowering my cunt onto his cock.

"Wine?" He hands me the nearly empty glass, and I finish it in a single swallow. I'm shaking and I can't tell if it's from the orgasm or my insatiable craving for more of Austin Wilder.

"We, uh, should get back. Don't you think?"

Though his debonair smile doesn't waver, I see the flicker of disappointment in his eyes. It twists my heart and nearly breaks my resolve—of which I have very little left of.

"If that's what you want."

I almost take his hand in mine, but I resist. The slightest physical contact between us is combustible, and I can't risk fueling the fire. "I've had a really nice time today. I mean that, Austin."

He starts to fill the picnic basket, that forced smile never leaving. It makes me feel terrible. I've never been one to get my fill of pleasure and run, but I can't expect him to believe that right now. "Let's get you back, then."

"Austin—"

"I like you, Liz. A lot. But I won't beg you to be with me."

Well, now I feel like an ass. Because I really do like him. More than I thought possible. But how do you tell someone you're afraid of falling *too* hard for them? It sounds like a lousy excuse to run away.

"I can't afford to lose focus on the bakery."

He nods but won't make eye contact with me anymore. "Don't worry about it. You didn't even buy the raffle ticket, right?"

"Austin, please stop." I grab for his wrist and latch on until he looks down at me. "I was honest from the start of this date." Yet I let the man play my pussy like a magic fiddle. Yeah, I'm terrible. I should've stopped things before they progressed that far. I'm ruined for every other orgasm in my future—namely ones I'll be giving myself.

"Maybe you can put me in your book then." He cracks a smile, attempting to break the awful tension that has spun up between us. I try to laugh, too. But it's forced so I stop. "Can you really deny there's something between us?" he asks.

No, I can't. That's why I have to leave while I still can. But the words don't find their way *out* of my mouth so he can hear them. I just stand there, mute.

Austin leans down and captures my mouth with his own. The kiss is hard and hungry. It's pointless denying my feelings for him. They're too powerful, and he's extracting the truth from me with this fiery kiss. "Tell me you didn't feel *that* and I'll let you walk out of my life."

He doesn't give me a chance to answer, just helps me onto my horse.

AUSTIN

The ride back to Liz's house is strained with uncomfortable silence. Mostly, I'm mad at myself. I should never have let things move so fast. Whatever pull exists between us is so much stronger than I ever imagined. Any sensible woman *would* be scared and run away. Hell, I'd already started planning our future and naming our kids when I was licking her juices off my fingers.

Until Liz, I never gave much thought to starting a family.

"Austin, I don't want this to be it," Liz says in her driveway. Her eyes are sad and pleading, and I'm forced to look away. "But I'm not ready to go all in. I'm not even ready for a relationship. This bakery really is important to me."

I want to kiss her again until she admits the truth —that she's afraid. But I'm not a jackass. "I don't want this to be it either, Liz. But I'm kind of an all or nothing guy."

"I can't offer you all right now."

Is it sad to cling to those two little words? *Right now*. Hope emerges deep in the recesses of my heart. We might have a future.

I squeeze her hand from the safety of the driver's seat. "I'm glad I met you."

"Me too." She slips out the truck and hurries to the front door as the last beams of sunlight fade. I should walk her to the door, but I can't. I'm scared that the woman I'm meant to be with might've just walked out of my life for good.

Before I can put the truck in reverse, my phone rings.

"Hey Tex," I say to my brother. "What's up?"

"We're thinking about getting on the road early. Colt has some interviews, and there's some famous all you can eat rib joint Hudson wants to try. Thought we might head out a couple days early. You in?"

I can't even remember where our next rodeo is at, but leaving town a couple of days ahead of schedule sounds great about right now. I need to get some space so I don't do something crazy, like show up at Liz's doorstep in the middle of the night and beg her to give us a chance. I've never been the begging kind, and I don't care to start now. "Means we leave tomorrow then?"

"Yeah."

"Count me in."

6

LIZ

"Why are you home?" Gemma demands the second the door closes behind me. "The sun literally just set three seconds ago. You were supposed to be watching it with a rodeo cowboy."

"The date's over," I say with as much nonchalance as I can muster. But deep down, I'm falling apart. I think I may have just made the biggest mistake of my life. What if letting Austin drive away tonight means I'll never see him again?

"What happened?"

It's too much to hope for privacy. Living with my sister means I can't send her away. "We had a nice time. The end." I strip out of my date clothes, leaving my bedroom door open. Gemma's going to barge in if I close it anyway.

"Are you going to see him again?"

I let out a heavy sigh. "Doubtful."

With folded arms, she barricades my exit. I plop down on my bed that's still buried in half my closet. "I was going to put those away later because I thought you'd be riding a cowboy tonight. Was he a jerk? I'll beat him up if he was."

I sputter a laugh. "I love you, Gem. No, he was not a jerk. Not even a little."

"Then what happened?"

I'm not ready to talk about the date yet, because I haven't finished processing it all. A part of me feels like it was all too fast, and another part of me knows it was right. *Meant to be.* I shake the irrational thought from my mind. "Can we put on a movie first? Talk after?"

"I've been saving a bag of M&Ms just for this occasion. I'll get the popcorn going." She opens her arms for a hug. As much as I'd love to wallow in self pity alone, I'm really glad I have Gemma to hang out with tonight.

The movie was a bad idea. Halfway through, tears are rolling down my cheeks because I want what the couple in the movie has. And dammit, I want it with Austin. But something is *still* holding me back from going after what I want.

Gemma lifts the remote and pauses the movie. "Ready to talk now?"

"I'm scared, Gem. Scared it's too fast. Too intense. Too crazy. What if I get sucked into this whirlwind relationship and lose sight of everything else? What if I never open the bakery because I'm too swept away with Austin and spend more time traveling to rodeos than actually making my own dream come true?"

"Did he ask you to give up your dream?" Her tone is neutral, but it packs a punch anyway.

"No."

"Then what are you *really* afraid of?"

I've been mulling over the answer to this question since the moment I asked Austin to take me home. Though I thought I knew the real reason, I know deep down it's a coverup for something grave. "Getting my heart broken." You don't get to fall hard for a man like Austin Wilder and recover from a breakup in any normal way. "I'm afraid losing him would destroy me."

"With the way that man looks at you, Liz, I bet you're wearing a ring in a month tops. *If* you go after him."

"But—"

"Look, breakups suck. But not giving someone special a chance ... is that *really* how you want to live your life? Because the Liz Hollingsworth I know isn't afraid of much. She's opening her own bakery, for crying out loud. I'm pretty sure she just learned how to ride a horse today, too."

"What do I do?" I don't have Austin's number, and I'm afraid that driving over to his ranch in the middle of the night might send the wrong message. I don't want him to think I'm there for some late-night booty call. I want him to know I'm ready to go all in.

"Use the skills the Lord blessed you with, honey. *Bake!*"

I practically tackle my sister in a hug. Pillows and popcorn go flying. "Gem, you're brilliant!"

AUSTIN

I'm tossing my duffle bag into the bed of my truck, ready to drive over to Tex's corner of the ranch when I see a tiny silver car speeding down the dirt road. We don't allow solicitors or uninvited guests on our ranch after some paparazzi snuck in a few years back. But I don't recognize the car or know why it's headed to *my* cabin.

I lean against the front of my truck and wait.

Despite the flying dust, those intense green eyes are hard to miss.

Liz.

She came back.

I swallow hard. Another ten minutes and I might've missed her completely. Though hope has suddenly burst inside me, I tamp down my excitement and keep my guard high. It felt wrong to sleep alone last night. Like half of me was missing. But I won't back down. If Liz can't go all in, I can't do this at all. Because once I'm inside her, she'll be mine forever.

"Are you leaving?" Liz's voice is softer and sweeter in person than from my dreams last night, of which there were plenty. Some delicious aroma sifts through the air. Maybe cinnamon? Whatever Liz is holding in her hands is hidden by a dish towel.

"Brothers and I were going to head to Tennessee a few days early," I say, dialing in my cool and casual demeanor I use so often at the rodeos. "Supposed to head out in a few minutes, actually."

"Oh." Her bright eyes dim and she nearly fumbles the covered dish in her hands. "If this is a bad time, I can go."

"Wait." The plea is out before I even have time to decide if I want to say the word. "You came all this way. The least I can do is hear you out." I fish my phone out of my pocket to let Tex know I need a few more minutes.

Liz lifts her dish in offering. "I brought cinnamon rolls."

Maybe I'll need more than a few minutes. "Why don't you come inside?" I take the dish from her, our hands grazing. The electricity from yesterday hasn't disappeared. In fact, it's amplified. If we go in through my door, I might not make the road trip with my brothers. In fact, I might have to fly just to get to the rodeo by the weekend.

"They're fresh out of the oven," Liz tells me as she follows me to the kitchen. "You should try one. See if I was telling the truth or not." There's that light flirty edge I've been missing.

I remove the towel, and the aroma that hits me is heaven. "Orgasm in my mouth, huh?" I give her a wicked smirk that lets her know *exactly* what I'm thinking as I take a generous bite. And holy shit, she's right. "Wow." I tear off another piece. "Liz, these are amazing."

"Told you."

I finish one roll—I don't want to be rude now—and go to wipe the frosting off my fingers. But Liz grabs my wrist to stop me.

"Let me."

She takes my fingers into her mouth and, one by one, sucks the frosting clean off. My dick presses against my zipper. I'm losing the will to resist her—and for the record I don't *want* to resist her—but until I know she's all in… "Liz." I take a step back. "Why'd you come here?"

"To apologize, for starters." She takes a step closer. "I'm sorry I ran away yesterday. I was afraid of what I was feeling between us. Afraid of getting hurt."

She feels it too.

I shoot Tex a message to let him know to leave without me. I'm not leaving this house until I've ravaged Liz in every single room. We're starting with the kitchen. "You're all in?"

"I'm all in, Austin."

7

LIZ

In a flat second, we're wrapped around each other in the middle of the kitchen. Hands desperate to roam our bodies, lips and tongues welded together, hips pressed hard against each other. It's no question how much Austin wants me right now. His hard length is pressed against my belly.

"I want you inside me, Austin."

His hands slide down my shoulders and stop on my boobs. Our lips break apart just a feather's distance. "Are you ready for what this will mean?"

I swallow hard. It means I'm making a commitment—a serious commitment with a man who has the power to shatter my heart. But he also has the power to love me in ways no one else could even dream of. I know that in the depths of my soul. "I'm ready."

In seconds, our clothes are scattered on the kitchen floor. His hand dives between my legs and teases my swollen bud. "So *wet* for me."

I wrap his massive cock in my hand and softly stroke him, pushing aside any rational fear about how he'll fit inside me. Deep down there's no question he'll fit perfectly. We're made for each other. If soulmates are real, he's mine.

Austin cups his hands under my ass and lifts me onto the counter like I weigh nothing. I should have all kinds of objections about having sex on the kitchen counter considering I'm a baker, but right now I don't care where we are or how we do it. I just need him inside me. I spread my legs in offering. "I need you, Austin. *Now*."

The counter proves to be the perfect height as he guides his cock to my entrance. He coats himself in my wetness before nudging his way inside. His hands shackle my hips and help me invite him in deeper and deeper.

I gasp at the sheer euphoria I feel when he's all the way seated. Everything feels right in this moment—*meant to be*. It's possible I'm even in love with this man. With his dark eyes penetrating my own, I'm sure he knows it too. I feel like he can see deep into my soul. I couldn't keep a secret from him if I wanted to.

Wrapping my legs around his hips and locking them with my ankles, we find a rhythm that feeds our hungry desire. He teases my clit with his thumb. It no time at all, I'm on the edge. Stars emerge behind my hooded eyes as pleasure consumes my entire body. I cry out his name as he thrusts into me over and over. I'm sensitive, but I don't want him to stop.

"Come inside me, Austin," I beg. "Claim me."

He thrusts hard three more times then holds me tight against him as he moans against my neck and his seed fills me. "You're mine now, Liz. No more running away."

"Never."

AUSTIN

My phone is filled with texts from all three of my brothers. I'm tempted to ignore them so I can take Liz into the bedroom. I'm not ready for either of us to put clothes back on yet. But if I don't reply, the whole gang might come knocking on the door.

"Just have to let my brothers know to head on without me today," I tell Liz after a long kiss. She's still on the counter, and I'm not ready to let her down yet.

"I don't want you to leave," says Liz, "but I know you have a job to do."

"They're going early. I have a couple of days before I have to get on the road myself. And I'm planning to spend as much of them as I can naked with you."

After a couple replies—mostly them giving me shit for being hung up on a girl—I set the phone down. It's then that I notice the distant look in Liz's eyes. I step between her legs, not surprised that I'm already growing hard again. I suspect that'll always be the case with this woman.

"What is it?" I ask.

"I love the idea of being naked with you for two whole days, but I also don't want to lose sight of what's important to me. I have a business plan to finish, and I'm supposed to meet a realtor tomorrow about a possible space to lease."

I cup her neck with both my hands and give her a delicate kiss. "I love you, Liz. I want to see you achieve your dreams. I promise not to keep you from anything important. I'll help you if you want me to. You just have to tell me what you need from me."

"You love me?"

"Completely."

"I never thought something so fast could feel so right. But it does. Maybe that's what scared me most of all. I love you, too, Austin. Very much." She draws me in for a kiss steamy enough to make my dick all the way hard.

"But I will need you naked for the better part of today."

"Done."

"Good. Now that that's settled, how do you feel about riding a cowboy?"

EPILOGUE

AUSTIN

"You ready to surprise Mommy?" I say to our daughter Sky.

"Yes!" Her green eyes—compliments of her mother—sparkle with excitement.

To say that I'm proud of my wife is an understatement. Liz Wilder has accomplished so much in the time that I've known her. She's not only opened her bakery, but she's had to expand and hire more employees to keep up with the high demands. Business is booming, and her cinnamon rolls are a top seller.

"Stay right here," I tell her as I move to shut off the lights. Today is Liz's birthday, and despite my insistence that she take the day off, she refused. So

Sky and I baked her a special surprise we found in an old recipe box.

My daughter stands on a stool behind the kitchen counter, and I stand behind her. I'd do anything to keep the girls in my life safe. Including our newest addition due in four months.

The deadbolt clicks open. "Shh," I tell Sky.

"Hello?" Liz calls out. "Anyone home?"

Sky is forced to muffle a giggle. She thinks this is the best and funniest thing she's ever been a part of. Soon, we're both laughing and fighting to hide it.

"I hear you guys," Liz calls.

The light flips on. "Surprise!" Sky and I yell in unison.

"What is this?" There are instant tears in Liz's eyes. Partially it's the hormones, but I know she's truly touched. Sky wants to grow up to be a baker just like her mom. I have to admit, the kid did a lot of the work. She has the knack.

"It's your birthday cake!" Sky announces. To this little girl, everything is exciting and thrilling. It's my favorite thing about her. She teaches me on a daily basis to be present and appreciate each and every moment.

"You guys didn't have to do that." Liz swipes at the tears and comes around the counter to give us a family hug.

"It's a special cake," I tell her. "All Sky's idea, though."

"It's a cinnamon roll cake!" Sky announces.

I shrug at her surprise. "We found one of your old recipes."

I give my wife a kiss that makes Sky wiggle free beneath us. "Happy Birthday, sweetheart." Against her ear, I whisper, "Tonight you'll get the rest of your present. Three or four times." I slide my hand between her legs when Sky turns her back to us, applying pressure as a promise of future pleasures.

"I can't wait," she says in a breathy whisper.

"Can we have cake? I want cake!" Sky demands, forcing us to save the naughty fun for later. "Cake!"

"Yes, sweetie," says Liz. "I can't wait to try your amazing cake!"

I'm so damn happy that this is my life.

TEX

WILDER BROTHERS RODEO BOOK 4

1

GEMMA

"When are you getting married, Gemma?" The Wilder brothers' Uncle Raine asks me as we wait for the rodeo stars to wrap up their interviews. This ritual after the rodeo has become my normal ever since my sister married into the Wilder family.

"Have to find the right man." The lie is easy enough to say. The truth though ... I *have* found the perfect one. He just doesn't know it yet.

Tex Wilder. I've had it *bad* for months now. Maybe longer. Ever since that day in the coffee shop when an elderly woman at the counter couldn't get her debit card to work. Tex stepped up and paid for her coffee. Not just for that day, but for the rest of the month.

Tex didn't notice me before he slipped out. But I never forgot his kind gesture.

"Sure you've been looking in the right places?" Raine asks with a teasing chuckle.

I like Raine a lot. He's like the wise, comedic uncle I never had. If anyone suspects my long, pathetic crush, it'd probably be him. "I'll find my knight in shining armor one of these days. You'll see." I pat him on the arm before I make a dash for the snack table to avoid where this conversation might lead.

He's only asking about my love life because my younger sister, Liz, just got married to Austin Wilder a few weeks ago. I scan the area again for my sister—she's the reason I've been coming to so many rodeos lately—but I think Liz is celebrating with her husband in private.

I've always known I wanted to marry a cowboy, ever since I was a little girl. But after Liz's wedding, I want it even more.

Tex Wilder is a mysterious, quiet man who keeps mostly to himself. He hasn't dated a woman in well over a year; not since his ex pulled some stunt no one's been willing to talk about. The only thing I've been able to figure out is she used Tex's fame for her own gain.

Though Tex is the entertainer for this particular rodeo circuit, he's also famous in other ways. He's played roles in a couple of big screen rodeo movies.

For that reason, he attracts the cameras more than his brothers. I've even heard a rumor that he's doing another movie. But rumors in this town can't always be trusted.

"Where is he?" I hear a shrill, female voice call above the crowd. "Tex? Honey?"

Honey?

My eyes narrow in search of the woman who dares lay stake to my claim. From what his brothers and uncle have let slip, Tex has no intentions of ever being in a relationship again. He didn't even bring a date to his brother's wedding.

"You should go," I hear Uncle Raine say to the woman.

Abandoning my snack plate, I weave my way through the small crowd to get a better look. Dammit, the woman is gorgeous. Elegant, flashy, and thin as a toothpick. She looks sorely out of place in the private grounds of a small town rodeo.

"Don't be silly. I'm not going anywhere without Tex. Where is he?"

"Gone home," I hear the oldest Wilder brother, Colt, pipe up. "Leave, Maxine. I won't tell him you stopped by."

The ex. It *has* to be.

"His truck's still here," she argues, folding both arms across her chest. The flimsy tank top she's wearing hardly hides anything. Not that she has much of a chest to hide. Not like mine. The thought makes me spurt a laugh, and her narrowed eyes shoot daggers at me.

"Who are *you*?"

Austin steps in front of me, protecting me like a big brother. "That's my sister-in-law," he says. Yep, my sister picked a good one. Even though she's the one who married into this family, they've accepted me as one of their own, too.

"What are you saying?" Maxine huffs.

It occurs to me that she might think I'm Tex's *wife*.

TEX

I make sure every bit of paint is off my face before I brave the after-rodeo crowd. I'm the entertainer that hangs out in the center of the ring to keep the crowd stimulated in between rides. I'm also a potential target for an angry bull during rides.

Uncle Raine is a godsend to bring his RV to every event so I have a place to shower when it's all over. It's not just the face paint, it's the dirt—and nights like tonight after a heavy rainfall—the mud. *So much mud.*

This weekend we're in our hometown, but that doesn't mean I want to muddy up my truck on the twelve mile ride home. Besides, I promised a local reporter I'd give a quick interview about my new movie role. So, here I am.

I stare at myself in the mirror, noticing the increasing number of lines around my eyes.

I'm getting older. No doubt about it.

If you'd asked me five years ago where I thought I'd be by now in life, this isn't quite it. Sure, I have some fame and I love the rodeo. But everything else I wanted—a wife, a family, and a house that felt like a home— has slipped out of my grasp. My heart's hardened too much.

During a rodeo, I'm outgoing and funny. The crowd *loves* me. But after, I'm quiet and reserved. I keep mostly to myself. Outside of my brothers, I don't have many people I'd call friends. It's just easier that way.

There was a time that wasn't the case. But betrayal has a way of turning a man cold.

"Let's just get this over with, huh?" I say to myself in the mirror, ripping my gaze away.

I stay to the shadows as much as I can, navigating my way around RVs and trucks to the pop-up tents. I've no doubt the reporter is at my family tent waiting for me, so I might as well grab a bite to eat before she pounces.

My heart skips a couple beats when I notice the gentle wave of Gemma Hollingsworth's dark red hair. She's surrounded by my brothers and uncle.

In another world, one where I wasn't so heartless and cold, I'd ask her out. Hell, I'd do a whole helluva lot more than that. But it's not fair to lure her in when I can't give her all the love she truly deserves. I'm a broken man, and she's an angel.

With a deep breath, I brave my way into the gaggle of family.

The roar of their voices grows louder with each step. Something's up. An upset fan? Or maybe a rival? Who'd Colt knock outta first?

I consider skipping out on the interview. Whatever's going on could be bad press captured by a hungry reporter, and I know myself too well. Exhausted, weary to my boots, my fuse is too short to hear someone slur our name. Raine can handle whatever it is. Austin too. I should just go.

But a shrill voice from my past lifts over the huddle and punches me square in the chest. "Where *is* he?" she demands, like it was for the fifth time.

Maxine.

The woman who betrayed me.

What the *hell* is she doing here?

2

GEMMA

"Maxine, it's time for you to leave," Austin says sternly, an unmoving barricade between me and *her*. Seriously, these Wilder brothers are like linebackers. I can hardly see around him.

"Not until I talk to Tex. Don't feed me some bullshit line about him being married to *her*, either."

The jab stings initially, but I brush it off. I may not be some cover model, but I love my curves. I *own* my curves. It's all I can do to keep myself from putting her in her place. I'm pretty sure one sweeping kick under her knees would knock her right off those stilettos and onto her bony little ass. Seriously, who wears high heels to a rodeo?

But the flash of a camera keeps me from pushing my way around Austin and playing out the fantasy in my head. The last thing I want is to be some headline in our local newspaper—or worse, the internet. I'm a high school teacher. I don't need my students or colleagues confronting me about a questionably violent headline. It might be summer break, but I run into someone from school almost daily.

"We can have security escort you out," Austin adds, adjusting his stance to block me completely from Maxine's sight.

I briefly wonder where my sister went off too when I notice something move in the shadows behind the open tent. There's a tall man with broad shoulders hiding in the cover of darkness behind the RV parked there.

Tex.

I don't need to catch the wafting of his woodsy cologne to know it's him. I can tell by the outline of that magnificent silhouette. I've practically memorized the lines of his muscular body. It's all that pining and watching from afar. Pathetic, I know. But I'm hung up on him. Bad.

As the arguing continues, I quietly slip backwards until I'm on the other side of the tent and free of the crowd. With extreme caution, I go to Tex.

My palms are sweaty, and my heart is racing faster than a fighter jet. But I force my voice to work so I can warn him. "Maxine," I say in a quiet voice, my eyes fill with both sympathy and longing. All I want is for this man to gather me in his arms. To claim me as his own.

But I know better.

"Great," he mutters, scrubbing a hand over the back of his neck. Even in the shadows, I see the strain in his dark eyes. "Do me a favor?"

"Anything." And I *do* mean anything.

"Don't tell them you saw me."

I swallow hard as I give him my nod of agreement. It's laughable how much I look forward to the nights after the rodeo is over. Tex is always the first to leave, but I cherish even the few minutes I get to be around him. When I have an ounce of courage, I even manage to pass off something like small talk with him.

"She's *not* married to him!" Maxine's high-pitched voice turns both our heads. It's hard to imagine Tex was ever with a woman like that. The physical part, I guess I understand. But she's bitchy and rude, even to his family. The Tex Wilder I've gotten to know the past year wouldn't tolerate that kind of behavior.

"I didn't tell her that." I lift my hands in surrender. "She just—"

"I know." Tex touches my bare shoulder with his rough, hot hand. Shivers assault my entire body at the contact. If anything ever did happen between us, I'd probably turn to ash after minutes together. I can't be imagining this insane level of chemistry between us. "She's up to something."

"You're not ... back tog—"

"Hell no."

"Then you should probably escape while you still can."

Tex nods, his hand sliding from my shoulder. I feel the absence of his touch immediately. "Right."

He's two strides away when the cameras start flashing.

"Tex Wilder, you get back here," Maxine orders. "We need to tell these fine reporters about our official engagement, honey." Though her voice is now sickeningly sweet, the shrillness is far from gone. Seriously, that woman could make nails on a chalkboard sound pleasant.

Before Tex can say anything, at least five different cameras blind us both. Reporters talk over one another, asking Tex if this is true.

"Of course it's not true."

Maxine tries to shove her way around me, as I'm the only one keeping Tex from being bombarded. But I block her path. *There's muscle in these curves, Barbie.*

After a death glare, she turns a smile back to the cameras. "We *are* engaged. Tex!" she calls over her shoulder at him. "It's okay, darling. We can tell them now."

Still not quite sure what this insane woman is up to, I do the only thing I can think of to help. Well, actually I don't think. I just act.

With cameras flashing, I close the distance between me and Tex, snake my hand around his neck, and kiss him right on the lips.

TEX

I'm taken by surprise at Gemma's impulsive gesture, but even my lips don't seem capable of being shocked. They're too busy moving against hers. As if it were the most natural thing in the world, my hands cradle her jaw and allow me better access to her mouth. She tastes of cinnamon. She moans, my tongue tangling with hers.

"Tex Wilder, are you with someone else now?" The scandal-hungry reporter's voice snaps me of the spell. I pull back from the kiss, but my hand cups Gemma's arm protectively.

She kissed me to save me.

"Don't be ridiculous!" Maxine bulls her way through, flames in her eyes. She wasn't always this ... intense. Hollywood hasn't been kind to her, or she wouldn't be desperate enough to show back up here. I'm not sure what she wants, but I can guess.

Protect Gemma. It's the only coherent thought I can sort out of this mess.

"I'm with Gemma," I say to the recorder shoved up in my face. "That's all you need to know."

"Tex! Tex!"

I have seconds to make my escape before this becomes ugly. *Our* escape. Maxine'll make a scene if I let her. She's never cared about what kind of press she gets, only that she gets it. I turn my back to the mob gathering behind us, protecting Gemma like a shield. "We have to go," I say.

"We?"

Whether she likes it or not, we're in this together now. I wouldn't dream of leaving her behind to the wolves. "Take my hand. We're making a run for it."

Gemma doesn't hesitate. Her fingers intertwine with mine, and I hustle us through a maze of vehicles on the way to my truck.

"The black one," I say, pointing to my truck a few yards away. A couple of reporters have gained on us, so it's a mad dash to the vehicle. Gemma and I just get inside and lock the doors as one of them reaches us. They tap on the glass as I crank the engine. Shifting gears, I spot Maxine glaring at me, broken heel in hand. How did I ever think I loved her?

"Buckle up."

Gemma doesn't say a word until we hit the paved highway. "Where are we going?"

If my ex wasn't involved in this shit-show, I'd drop Gemma off at her house and head back to my cabin on the Wilder ranch. But my companion is no longer safe from nosey reporters, and Maxine will certainly raid the ranch. I turn to Gemma and take her hand in mine. "Do you trust me?"

"Yes." The quickness of her answer surprises me. "You shouldn't."

Gemma lets out an easy laugh that lifts some of the tension of the pursuit we just experienced. "What are you going to do, Tex Wilder? Take me to some remote place and have your way with me?" With the glow of the moonlight and dashboard lights, the mischievous twinkle in her eyes is unmistakable.

I don't dare tell her that very thought has crossed my mind. Especially after that heated kiss. I've wondered a dozen times already how far that kiss would've gone had it just been the two of us in the shadows without any prying eyes.

"Be careful what you wish for, Gemma." I mean it as a tease, but my words come out far more serious than that. "I have a remote cabin, off the main ranch. No one knows about it but me. Not even my brothers."

"We're going there?"

"Yes. Do you need to call Liz?"

"I'll text her. Let her know I'm with you." With her head tucked down toward her phone, I admire the soft wave of her long hair. My eyes linger too long on the edges of it brushing against her voluptuous chest. If only Gemma knew how much I've wanted her, she wouldn't dare be alone with me now. It's going to be a long night in a small cabin.

3

GEMMA

I've never seen so many stars in my life before. The sky seems to stretch forever, painted in entire galaxies. It's simply breathtaking.

But it *is* remote. Not a soul, or even a porchlight, around for miles.

"I know it looks a little scary, but it's safe. I promise," Tex says before we get out of the truck. "And not just from reporters."

I wonder if he means coyotes and mountain lions. Or him.

"No one knows about this place?" A sensible person might be worried, but I'm just a ball of nerves. Tex isn't exactly a stranger. I've been around him and his family for over a year. Ever since my sister started dating Austin. But Tex is still very much a mystery to me. One I hope to unravel tonight without making a complete fool out of myself.

"Nope."

"Not any of your brothers? Or Uncle Raine?"

Tex lets out an easy laugh as he takes my hand and leads me to the covered front porch. "Are you kidding? They'd be up here all the time if I told them about this place. A man needs some secrets, even from his family."

"But now I know your secret."

He opens the door, reaches around for a light switch, and waves me inside. I wasn't sure if the place had electricity until now. "Consider yourself special, Gemma Hollingsworth."

I've had a lot of special days in my life—the first day I started teaching, the first day a student told me I was their favorite—but this might take the cake. For months, I've pined for time alone with Tex. Time away from eavesdroppers and fans.

Who knew all I had to do was kiss the man to get it?

"I trust you'll keep my secret," Tex says to me, his tone serious.

I gulp a swallow, meeting those dark, intense eyes. "Of course you can trust me." My nipples pebble, and I drop my gaze. If I don't keep myself occupied, I might do more than kiss him. I'd never live down the humiliation if Tex Wilder rejected me.

"How long have you had the place?" I slowly wander the open concept kitchen and living area. The furniture is sparse, but the framed pictures on the wall are plentiful.

"Bought it last summer."

"Wow, you're pretty good at keeping secrets then."

Tex moves toward the fridge, opening the door and poking his head inside. "I don't have much," he says. "Some beer. Bottled water. Can't say I trust the orange juice."

I stop in front of a framed picture from a movie set I recognize. Tex has been in three different films, and I've watched them all so many times I have everyone's lines memorized. "I'd be up for a beer."

I hear the crack of two bottles caps, but not the approaching footsteps that would have warned me about his proximity. "Here you go."

"Thanks." Our fingers brush against each other as he hands me a cold bottle, and I'm instantly transported back to that steamy kiss. Tex didn't freeze under my impulsive move. His lips moved right along with mine, almost like he *wanted* to kiss me. I want so badly to ask him, to know if maybe, just maybe, Tex Wilder might be into me.

"This is from my first movie," he says with a nod toward the framed photo I'm admiring.

"I know."

"Do you?"

"Who in this town doesn't know about your movie star status?" I tease.

"Just minor roles," he says. "I'm nobody."

Did I imagine the hurt in his voice? I turn to him and dare to gaze into the depths of his eyes for the answer. It's a dangerous thing to do, and I might live to regret it. "You're *not* nobody, Tex." I want to tell the man he's everything. I almost do. But fear holds me back. If things get awkward between us, we're stuck together. "Everybody loves you. Not just the actor version. The entertainer."

He shrugs a laugh. "That's acting too, sweetheart." Tex steps away and takes a drink. The electric cloud between us thins, but I feel pulled to him just the same. I fight the urge and take a sip from my own bottle.

I continue to roam until I reach a short hallway. The bedroom door is wide open, and the moonlight pouring in from the window reveals a large bed. I can't seem to tear my eyes away. Surely it's safer to stare at a piece of furniture than the cowboy behind me.

"To be safe, we should stay the night," Tex says from the opposite side of the kitchen island. "Will that be a problem?"

TEX

. . .

"Nope. No problem here." Gemma still hasn't turned around from the hallway, which means I still haven't stopped staring at her ass. The urge to grab her is so overwhelming I have to force myself to put distance between us.

"There's no cell reception out here," I add. It's the last out I'm giving her. I'm drawn to Gemma in ways I shouldn't be. She's too sweet for a broken cowboy. The last thing I want to do is destroy her.

"I told Liz I was with you," she says, finally turning toward me.

My eyes sweep over her curves, practically making me salivate. For months I've fantasized about stripping Gemma down naked and kissing every inch of her body. Desire for her has tugged at me in my dreams. Would it scare her to know that I stroked myself to her image in the shower just this morning?

Fuck me. I need to do something—anything—to distract myself from misbehaving. "What's your story Gemma?" I ask, going to the fridge for a second beer.

"My story?"

"Yeah. Where'd you grow up? What do you do? That sort of thing."

Gemma slips onto a barstool on the opposite side of the island and leans against the counter. It's impossible not to admire the generous cleavage on display.

"Grew up here," says Gemma. "Born and raised. Both of my parents have passed away. My younger sister Liz is my only remaining family. I'm a high school drama teacher." She shrugs, her finger circling the rim of her bottle. "I guess that's kind of all there is to tell."

I should leave it alone. The more I get to know about Gemma, the harder it will be to resist her. But I can't help myself. "What's your favorite childhood memory?"

"Oh, that's an easy one," she says. "My family took a trip to Universal Studios in Hollywood. I was nine at the time. It was the most magical experience of my life. It's the reason I became a drama teacher, really."

"You like acting."

Gemma leans back, but it doesn't help distract me from her tits. Fuck this is going to be a long night.

"I like the possibly of being someone else for a little while," she answers. "It's fun. Wouldn't you agree?"

Though my movie roles have all required me to be a cowboy, they definitely did allow me to become someone else entirely. "I guess."

Gemma empties her beer. I envy the bottle that got to feel her lips pressing against it. That kiss is on replay in my mind. I want to kiss her again, but I know where it'll lead. Straight to a heartbroken Gemma. "We should get some sleep," I say. "It's late."

She slips off her stool and comes around the kitchen island to rinse out her bottle in the sink. Our hips brush and my breath hitches. "Only one bed, huh?" She's staring into the sink, so I can't see the expression on her face.

"I can sleep out here."

"Where?"

"On the couch."

Gemma laughs. "It's a loveseat. It's way too short."

When I picked out the furniture for this place, I never intended to have a guest. It was perfect for one man. "Take the bed, Gemma." The mattress is only a full size.

"We're adults, Tex. We can both sleep in the bed and behave ourselves. Right?"

"Right." But it's a lie. How the hell will I keep my hands to myself with Gemma sleeping right beside me?

4

GEMMA

"You never wanted to be a bull rider?" I ask Tex from my spot on the bed. Despite our best attempts to sleep, it's been impossible. Neither of us are tired, and the sexual tension is swirling like a cyclone in the short gap between our bodies.

"Nah. Those guys are nuts."

We both laugh, as we've done many times while lying here together. It's ... comfortable. I'm still nervous as hell and hornier than I think I've ever been in my entire life, but propped on my side with Tex across from me in the moonlit room feels natural.

"Your turn," I say to Tex. Once we determined

neither of us were going to sleep easily, we decided to swap questions.

"What would you be if you could be anything?"

The truth is, I'm pretty happy being me. Maybe to some people, being a high school drama teacher isn't that exciting. I know it's my calling, and I'm damn good at it. But in effort to keep things fun and lighthearted, I give Tex a different answer. "I always thought it might be fun to be a famous actress. Pretend to be someone different every movie. Strut down the red carpet. Have more money than I'd ever know how to spend."

"It's not all glitz and glamour," Tex says, the smile dropping from his lips.

"It's just a fantasy, Tex." I daringly reach my hand out and use the tips of my fingers to lift his frown into a smile. I had hoped to make us laugh, but instead we're both breathing heavier.

I wait for him to tell me to ask the next question. Instead, he takes my hand into his own and brings my fingers to his lips.

My panties were soaked hours ago, but my center tingles with urgency. I've spent so many nights tossing and turning, wishing Tex were in my bed with me.

And here he is.

To feel the brush of his lips against my skin is riveting. He kisses my fingers once more then pushes my hand back toward me. "Gemma, you're a very special woman."

I cringe, my heart sinking. I've heard this line before. "Thanks?"

He sits up, those dark eyes peering down at me. "I'm a broken man. I can't offer you what you want."

It's embarrassing how quickly hot tears assault the corners of my eyes. Of course Tex Wilder isn't interested in me that way. If he was, it wouldn't have taken him a year and an isolated cabin to admit it. I roll off the bed and hurry out of the room, swiping at the stupid tears.

"Gemma," he says.

Since leaving isn't an option tonight unless I want to walk several miles, I'll sleep on the loveseat. I gather the throw blanket from the top of the couch cushion. It's small, but it'll keep me from freezing.

"Gemma, stop."

"It's fine, Tex," I reply without turning around. I *won't* let him see me cry. "Just go to bed."

The familiar woodsy cologne surrounds me at his approach. "Gemma, I didn't mean it like that." His hands cup my shoulders and turn me toward him, but I refuse to look up into those eyes.

"Of course you did." I try to shimmy out of his grip but fail. Even embarrassed as I am right now, the heat of his touch is doing all sorts of things to my body. Every nerve ending is awake. "I'm not your cover model type, and it's okay. Let's not make this any more awkward than it already is." Hopefully I can skip a couple of rodeo weekends and things will go back to normal.

Hopefully.

"You really think that's what this is about?"

Like an idiot, I meet his gaze. I'm snared in a trap. So many emotions swirl in his eyes it'd take a lifetime to unravel them all. "What else would it be?"

"All I want is to kiss you again, Gemma. Every last inch of you."

My eyes widen at his declaration. Because I've been unable to look away from him, I can see the sincerity of his words. "Then what's stopping you?"

TEX

Desire is pulsing through every vein in my body for Gemma. I've noticed her since the first time I saw her, more than a year ago in a local coffee shop. I didn't even say hello to her then, and I've always regretted it.

But the heartache was very real back then. I knew I couldn't trust myself not to hurt someone else when I was so badly mangled, so very black inside. I'm still mangled, but Gemma's presence makes me feel hopeful that I'm mending somehow.

"You deserve someone who can love you with his whole heart. I don't have a whole heart."

Gemma steps closer and reaches a hand to my cheek. "Then let me help you make it whole again."

Resisting her kiss would be futile. Like refusing air to breath. I gather her into my arms and devour her mouth, finishing what we started at the rodeo. I kiss her until we're both heaving and out of breath. Then I move my lips along her neck.

Her fingers dig into the back of my head as I move lower.

I slide my hands down her back until they're cupped on her ass. In one swoop, I lift her up and she puts her legs around my waist. I carry her to the bedroom and set her on the edge of the mattress. "I meant what I said. I want to kiss *every* inch of you."

Though I'm eager to have her, I force myself to go slow. I remove her jeans with agonizing leisure, kneeling before her as I shimmy them from her ankles and onto the floor. I kiss my way up one leg and down the other.

"You're going to kill me," she says.

"I've wanted you too long to rush this."

"What?"

I lift her shirt over her head, not shy at all about running my hands over the sides of her tits. "Did you think I didn't notice you and this hot body of yours?" I kiss her nipples through the fabric of her bra.

"Why would you notice me?"

I lock my gaze with hers. "Because you're the most amazing woman I've ever had the pleasure of meeting."

"You've hardly ever talked to me."

Unclasping her bra, I urge her to lie down. "I never felt worthy of you, Gemma." I grab a tit in each hand and start my not-so-gentle massage, kissing a trail between them. "If you think I've never thought about being inside you, you're wrong. I've wanted you for so long."

"I've wanted you, too."

A part of me has known this to be true for months. The part of me that was pretty damn good at denial. I take my time kissing my way down to her panties. Slowly, I peel those away too. "I don't want to hurt you, Gemma. I'd never forgive myself if I did."

"You didn't even stay long enough at the wedding to dance with me," she says. From between her legs, I watch the heavy rise and fall of her tits. "I was going to ask you."

"I'm sorry I didn't stay." My lips trace a line along the inside of her thighs. "Please, let me make it up to you." The sweet scent of her pussy has been teasing me long enough. I spread her lips and stroke her slowly with my tongue. Gemma gasps and fists a hand in my hair.

"First," I say against her swollen nub, "I'm going to eat your sweet, sweet pussy." Her hips buck against my mouth. I know the vibration of my voice is adding an extra layer of pleasure. "And when I'm done, sweetheart, I'm going to do what I've wanted to do since the first time I saw you." She's moaning louder, panting heavier. "I'm going to bury my cock deep inside you and claim you for myself."

5

GEMMA

The vibrations of Tex's mouth against my pussy are insane. His tongue and his mouth are working some form of magic down there. An alarming number of moans and cries escape from my mouth, but I don't care.

Tex freaking Wilder is eating me out.

The sinfully hot cowboy got *me* naked. He's wanted *me* all this time. If this is some fantasy dream, I hope I never wake up.

I feel a finger slip inside my channel, and my hips buck toward his mouth on reflex.

"That's it, Gemma," he says with his mouth fused to my cunt. "Rock that pussy."

In all of my fantasies, I don't think I've pictured

anything as hot as this scene right here, with Tex between my legs. I do as he says and gyrate my hips against his mouth as his finger slides in and out of me. With the hand I've had fisted in his hair since this all started, I push him harder against me.

His greedy laugh buzzes against my increasingly sensitive bud. My eyelids keep trying to fall closed, but I fight it. I want to watch him devour me as I near the edge. I cry out his name as an orgasm consumes every nerve ending in my body.

"I could do that all night," I hear Tex say as I feel the weight of him climb up the bed. Somewhere in that explosion, my eyes clamped shut. But now that they're open, I see that Tex is missing his clothes. "But I have other things in mind."

He straddles me, revealing himself to me as he sits on his bent legs. Holy shit that man is packing. I've always imagined Tex was well-endowed but I had no freaking idea he was so massive. Precum glistens against the moonlight. "Do you want me to use protection?" he asks. Still, I can't peel my gaze away from his hard length.

"I'm on the pill. There's been no one, Tex. Not in years. I've been waiting ... for you."

Lifting my ass, he sets me on his thighs. "There's no turning back from this, Gemma. You'll belong to me. Are you ready for what this means?"

"I've been ready."

He uses his hand to rub his dick through my

soaked pussy, coating himself in my wetness before setting me back on the bed. Lowering himself and hovering on top of me, Tex lines his cock up with my entrance. I feel his tip nudge my opening. "Tell me how you want it, Gemma."

My nipples tingle with excitement at such a dirty question. "Don't hold back. I want it all." I wrap my legs around his lower back and lock my ankles as he sinks his entire length into me at once.

I'm certain I've gone blind. The shock of his size is riveting through me, but I feel complete. Tex pulls out and plunges back in, giving me exactly what I asked for. I rock my hips in rhythm, meeting him with each thrust. I'm still sensitive from my first orgasm, but I feel another building.

Every smile, every accidental brush against each other, every stolen moment of conversation flashes through my mind as the wave of pleasure builds and builds. I've been in love with Tex Wilder for what feels like forever. I want to tell him how I feel. I want to confess my true feelings while he's inside me, closer to me than he could ever get.

But something holds me back.

Fear. Always fear.

"Come inside me, Tex. Please come inside me," I plead, wanting that one last thing to cement this most intimate moment. I don't know what tomorrow will bring, but I don't want to leave with any regrets.

"Come with me," he orders, pumping faster. He

shackles my hips with his hands and goes harder until we both explode together.

TEX

I know my heart is not whole, but as I release myself inside Gemma, I know she can help me become whole again. The truth I've been denying for so long is more evident now than ever. Gemma Hollingsworth is meant to have a permanent place in my life.

"I can't believe I waited so long," I say once we both catch our breath and I drop onto my back beside her.

She turns her head toward me and gives me a sultry smile. "It was worth the wait. I won't be able to walk for two days."

"Better bank on four or five then, because we are *not* done." I draw her into my arms. She nestles her head against my chest, and nothing has ever felt more right in my entire life. I'm repulsed at myself for ever getting involved with my ex when Gemma has been right here in my hometown this entire time.

Why didn't I meet her earlier in my life?

"I wish we could stay out here," Gemma says as

she traces soft circles on my chest. "Forget about reality for a while. This is kind of nice, you know?"

"Me too. But besides the fact we'd starve, they'd send a search party if we're out of touch too long." I brush the hair from her cheek and tuck it behind her ear. The sight of her bare tit resting against my abdomen, nipple hard, is possibly the sexiest thing I've ever seen. "I'll take you to breakfast in the morning. There's a diner I love in a tiny town most people don't even know exists."

"That sounds perfect."

For the first time in at least a couple of years, I finally feel like the future I always dreamed of having might actually be possible. My dick starts to harden again, imagining lying in bed with Gemma every night. *Naked.*

Her fingers slide down my stomach.

My dick twitches in anticipation.

When her soft, small hand closes around my cock, I suck in a breath. It takes nothing for me to be hard again with her precious fingers working their magic. "How do you want it?" she asks me.

I want her in every position, every way possible. How the hell can I choose just one now?

"Do you want me to bend over?" she asks. "Or I could ride my cowboy?"

The way she says *my cowboy* wins me over. I like the sound of it so damn much. "Better saddle up and hold on tight," I say. "It's going to be a wild ride."

6

GEMMA

"How many people does this little town have in it?" I ask as Tex parks his truck outside the cutest diner I've ever seen. It's like a flashback straight to the fifties with its chrome siding and checker patterned everything.

"Less than two hundred, by official count." He squeezes my hand. "Ready to get some breakfast?"

The smile I give him spreads throughout my entire body. Never in a million years would I have thought Tex Wilder would really want to be with me when he can have his pick of any woman. I'm still afraid someone will shake me awake from this wonderful dream. "I'm starving."

The hostess, who's also apparently the only

server, greets Tex warmly. Like he's an old friend. I suspect he comes here a lot. But the woman, old enough to be his mother, doesn't moon over him like he's a celebrity. She treats him like a regular guy. I bet it's refreshing.

"If you like pancakes," Tex says as he waits for me to slip into the booth seat then slides in beside me, "they make the best blueberry ones you'll ever eat." Tex drapes his arm around me, pulling me tight against him.

The words *I love you* have been begging to leave my lips since last night. They almost escape now.

"What can I get you two to drink?" The hostess asks. "Coffee? Orange juice?"

"Orange juice," we say in unison. As if I needed another reason to smile. Forget my legs being wobbly and sore. By the end of the day, my cheek muscles won't function.

"Coming right up."

Tex kisses me when she walks away, making my toes curl and my nipples tingle. If we were alone, I'd do him right here in this booth. I thought having sex with him last night would calm down my cravings for a while, but they've only intensified.

"You're really special to me, Gemma. I want you to know that."

I kiss him again to avoid blurting out my undying love. I'd never forgive myself if my confession scared him away hardly a day after being with him. "Rumor has it you're doing another movie soon. Is that true?"

"Yeah, my agent twisted my arm."

"Can you tell me what it's about, or is that top secret?"

"It's a movie about a bull rider and the woman he almost loses over his own stupidity. I'm playing that guy's brother. The one who stays home and takes care of the failing ranch that's in desperate need of his winnings."

I can't deny how exciting it is to get firsthand knowledge from Tex Wilder himself about his next movie role. I wonder if he'll do more. If we'll have conversations like this one in this very diner. Or will he talk to me about a role he's been considering as we lounge naked in bed? *Get a hold of yourself, Gemma. You've been together like six minutes.*

As we eat the best blueberry pancakes I've ever tasted, Tex tells me more about the movie role, his childhood, and funny rodeo stories. I still feel like a circus of butterflies is performing in my stomach around him, but I'm relaxing more and more.

Could this really be my future? *Our* future?

"I need to get some gas before we head back," he says, pulling alongside a gas pump. "We won't make it back otherwise."

"I'm going to run inside and grab something to drink. Want anything?" I ask.

"Bottle of water for the road would be great."

The gas station has the tiniest convenience store I've ever seen, but there is one cooler filled with water and soft drinks. Beside the cooler I spot a magazine stand. It's mostly tabloids, which I never read—nothing in them can be trusted. But one headlines pulls me back before I make it to the counter: *Has Tex Wilder Found Love with Gemma Hollingsworth?*

With shaky fingers, I pull the tabloid from the stand. I'm afraid of what it says, of what consequences might come with it. For a fleeting second, I regret what I did last night. But then I see the photo they captured. Tex and I are kissing.

I snatch a copy off the rack so I can read the article later. Better to be armed with knowledge than caught blindsided. After I pay for our waters, I stuff the magazine into my purse and return to the truck.

"Ready to face the music?" Tex asks me.

"Guess we have to at some point, huh?"

TEX

"Next weekend I'll be in San Antonio," I say to Gemma as we reach the outskirts of town. In minutes, I'll have to drop her off at her house. We haven't talked about what happens next, but I know

I want her in my life. "Do you want to come with me?"

"To the rodeo in Texas?"

"Yeah. As my girlfriend." Someday sooner rather than later, she'll be my wife. "School hasn't started yet, so I thought we might take the scenic route and drive together."

"I'd like that."

We arrive at her house much too soon. The only upside is that reporters aren't hovering outside her house. "I'll call you," I say, reluctant as hell to let her out of my sight. "I have to make sure my ex has packed up and left town. I don't want to drag you into that shit-show any more than you've already had to be."

"Walk me to my door?"

I do more than that. I come inside for what is supposed to be a brief moment. A simple goodbye kiss that we can finish later tonight. But before either of us knows what happens, Gemma is backed up against the wall and my hand is shoved up her shirt.

"Do you have time for a quickie?" She's biting her bottom lip, and it's making it really hard to say no. So I don't.

We fumble our way to the back of the couch before I yank her pants down to her knees. Her panties were lost somewhere in my cabin, so she's not wearing any. I lift her and prop her ass on top of the back of her couch as she unzips my jeans.

Within seconds, my cock is buried deep inside the place it most belongs.

"Harder," she begs. "Harder, Tex."

I slam my cock inside over and over until we're both crying out. I will never get tired of fucking this woman. Never.

I kiss her hard on the mouth. "I'm sorry I have to rush out—"

"Go, take care of things. You know where I'll be."

I love how understanding and calm she is about such a twisted situation. After today, I hope to be rid of my ex forever. I don't want her ever trying to come between us, even though I know she would never succeed. Gemma is too smart for that.

"I lo—" I stop myself before I blurt out a confession I'm not ready to share. I think I might be in love with Gemma. But until I'm sure, I don't want to say those special words out loud. "I'll call you soon."

In the midst of our passionate tumbling around, we dropped things and knocked others over. I spot her purse, spilled over on the floor.

"Don't worry about the mess," she says to me as she shimmies her jeans back over her curvy hips. "I'll take care of it."

I'm at the door when I see the tabloid sprawled out beside her purse. Our picture is plastered on the front, and the headline includes both our names. I bend over to pick it up, a familiar old rage bubbling inside me. I don't want to believe it. Gemma is different. I believed she was different. "Why do you have this?"

"I saw it in the gas station. I just wanted—"

"You want to be actress." The clues I've been ignoring this entire time are falling into place.

"That was just a fantasy, Tex."

"You kept asking me about my movie role…" I crush the tabloid in my balled-up fist. I need to leave before my anger consumes me. "I thought you were different, Gemma. But turns out you're just like her, looking for your shot at my expense."

I feel the ice hardening over my heart as I let the door slam behind me. How could I have been so stupid?

7

GEMMA

There isn't enough ice cream in the state of Montana to mend my broken heart, but that hasn't stopped me from testing the theory. Three empty cartons from the past three days line my kitchen counter.

"Have you eaten *anything* else?" Liz asks.

"Ice cream is the only thing that makes me happy."

She pulls me into a hug and doesn't let go, even though I must smell like a dump truck. I haven't showered in three or four days. It's pitiful, but I don't want to wash Tex away. I'm not ready to say goodbye over some stupid misunderstanding. But the man won't take my calls or answer my texts.

"If he doesn't believe you, Gemma, then he's not the one for you."

The sobs are instant at that declaration, because if Tex Wilder isn't the one for me, I'm doomed to be alone the rest of my life. No man will ever come close. "I don't want to be a stupid actress!"

"Then why did you say you did?"

"We were talking about fantasies. The *fantasy* of being famous is nice. But I don't really want that. I'd never put in that much work for a few ridiculous benefits. I love *teaching* acting." I'm mad at myself for not telling Tex that when I had the chance.

"Look, he's an asshat if he thinks you're anything like that awful ex of his. I love the Wilder clan like they're our second family, but even good families have rotten eggs sometimes." She pulls me down the hall by the arm, stopping outside the bathroom door. "Now, you're going to shower. Maybe you should burn those clothes."

"Liz!"

"Kidding. I'm kidding." She shoves me inside the bathroom and pulls the door closed. "Get cleaned up. Then you're coming over for dinner. Austin and I have news to share."

TEX

. . .

The last thing I want to do is attend some family dinner tonight, but I force myself to shower and put on clean clothes for my brother's sake. Austin told me he and his wife have news to share, and they want the entire family over to hear what it is.

Fine. I'll be there. Do the family thing tonight. Cause tomorrow, I'm hitting the road for San Antonio. Alone. I hope the drive will do me some good, but I don't have high expectations. I thought my heart would harden over again, like it did when Maxine ripped it out. But the damn thing's still bleeding like it'll never run dry.

All I can think about is Gemma. She's in every dream, every thought, every breath I take.

A pounding at the door warns me I'm running behind. Austin and Liz's cabin is the closest one to mine—walking distance if I take the dirt trail. "Coming," I call out when the pounding repeats. Snagging my keys, I join him on the porch.

"You *are* dressed," my oldest brother Colt says with a nod of approval. "Here I thought I'd have to hose you off and drag you over my shoulder."

"Very funny." I lock the door behind me—something I hadn't worried about doing in months until Maxine showed up last weekend. Luckily, she gave up and left town after the reporters didn't even mention her name in the tabloid article.

"You made a mistake," Colt says halfway down the trail.

"Excuse me?"

"You heard me. You're wrong about Gemma. So, get your head out of your ass and fix it before it's too late." Colt leaves me standing at the edge of the path, lost for words. My first instinct is to argue, but deep down I know he's right.

Colt is through the front door of Austin's house before my feet move again. It takes less than three strides for me to see that wavy dark red hair through the window. *Gemma's here.* I glance over my shoulder, wondering how fast I can run back to my place and drive away in my truck.

"Don't even think about it," Colt calls from the front door. "Get your ass inside. We're hungry."

My heart stops in my chest at the sight of Gemma. She's more beautiful than I remember, but the dimness in her eyes twists me inside. *I* did this to her. I stole her bright smile. I'm such an idiot to think she was anything like Maxine. I don't know why she had that tabloid, but it doesn't matter. I love her.

"Thank you everyone for coming," Liz says once Austin gets everyone to quiet down. The living room is packed with all the Wilders, including the youngsters. My nephew Conner tugs on Colt's sleeve. That kid is the spitting image of Colt.

I want a family. With Gemma.

"We have an announcement to make," Liz says. "And then we'll eat. I promise!"

Austin puts his arm around his wife, and it reminds me of the wedding I left early. The one where Gemma was going to work up the courage to ask me to dance. But I didn't give her the chance. What if I'd just stayed a little longer? Would our story have begun without flashing cameras and all the drama that entailed?

"We're having a baby!"

The room erupts in cheers and hoots. I manage to clap my hands together and force a smile. I'm truly happy for them, and later I'll tell them. But right now, my sights are set on Gemma. I'm going to fix this.

I weave around the furniture and kiddos darting around the room like a pinball in play. I grab for Gemma's hand a second before she turns for the kitchen. "Gemma, wait."

She stares at our connected hands but her expression remains unreadable and blank. "What do you want, Tex?"

"Can we go outside a minute to talk?"

Her eyes slowly lift until they meet mine. The pain lingering there makes me want to die. "I don't know."

"Please?"

She looks around the room, no doubt searching for her sister. But when her gaze stops on Liz, who's busy hugging Hudson and his wife Jillian, she lets out a deep sigh. "Sure." She pulls her hand free and walks toward the front door.

The moment we're outside and out of earshot from the open windows, I say, "I'm sorry, Gemma. I'm so damn sorry. I know you're nothing like her."

Gemma folds her arms across her chest. "I *am* nothing like her."

"I froze when I saw that tabloid in your purse. It didn't make any sense to me at the time. But I'm a fool, Gemma. I want to fix this. I want to make it right."

"I don't know."

My heart is cracking in two. If Gemma walks away, I know I'll never recover from the blow. "I love you."

Her dropped head snaps up and she stares at me with wide eyes. "Don't you dare say those words unless you mean them, Tex Wilder."

The slightest ray of hope shines in my soul and I close the distance between us. "I *do* love you, Gemma. I love you so much it scares me. My life won't be complete without you in it. I don't just want to roll around with you naked—though that is admittedly one of my favorite things to do."

Her cheeks heat to a pink color.

"I want a future with you, Gemma. I want us to be the ones making that announcement someday. I want a family."

"What are you saying?"

Though I wasn't planning to ask this tonight and I'm unprepared, I drop to one knee. "I've been drawn to you since the first time I saw you in that coffee shop. A part of me has known this whole time you were meant to be my wife. I don't care why you kissed me that first time, but I'm glad you did. I love you Gemma Hollingsworth. Will you marry me?"

Tears drop from her eyes as her hands cover her mouth in shock.

Though my family can't hear us, a bunch of them are watching this play out. I see them gathered in the dining room window. "Gemma?"

"Yes." She finally drops her hands.

"Yes?"

"Yes, I'll marry you."

I leap up, wrapping my arms around her waist and lifting her in the process. I spin us both in a circle as her lips descend on mine. Cheers and whistles echo faintly from the house.

"I love you, too," she says to me. "I've loved you for so long. I wanted to tell you, out at the cabin. But I was afraid."

I kiss her again, and all the pent-up feelings of the last few days emerge. I missed her so damn much I could hardly sleep. "Will you still come to San Antonio with me tomorrow? As my fiancé?"

"Of course I will."

EPILOGUE

GEMMA

"That's daddy!" Jared, our three-year-old son shouts with excitement, pointing to the TV.

"Yes it is, sweetie." I hug my little boy tight, thankful he's still at that age where snuggling Mom is cool. Tonight, it's just me and my kid, as Tex is in California shooting another movie. He was offered the lead role, but turned it down for a minor one so he'd be gone less.

"I'm not trying to become a big movie star you know," he told me before he left last week. "I just want to take care of my family."

We watch the movie until the very end, and Jared gets excited each time Tex comes on screen. We've made it a game to watch for Daddy's name when the credits role, but tonight my little man is yawning worse than the Big Bad Wolf.

"Time for bed, bud." Jared only gives me a mild fit tonight, for which I'm thankful.

I'm proud of Tex, but I miss him too. Sleeping in my bed alone isn't my preference.

Once Jared is tucked in and fast asleep, I clean up our popcorn bowls in the living room. I check my phone once more, hoping to hear from Tex before I turn in for the night. I'll never understand the hours some actors work.

"Nothing, huh?" I try not to let disappointment set in as I type out a text to him: *I love you*.

"I love you, too."

I let out a tiny scream at the sound of his voice so near. "Tex! What are you doing here? And why are you sneaking in? You scared me half to death!" I should stay mad, especially because I just got Jared to sleep. But I'm too happy to see him to stay upset.

"We wrapped up filming early." He gathers me in his arms and kisses me hard on the mouth. The week apart has felt like a year, and all that missing each other is wrapped up in this very heated kiss.

"Why didn't you tell me you were coming home?"

"And spoil the surprise?" Tex kisses my neck as his hands slide to my ass. He yanks my hips against his. I feel his erection through his jeans. "Why don't you and I go roll around in our bed?"

"Naked?" I ask with a devious smile. It's been almost four years, and I still want my husband as bad as the day I first had him.

"Is there any other way?"

STAY IN TOUCH!

Sign up for Kali Hart's newsletter to stay up to date on new releases, giveaways, and more!
http://eepurl.com/gHPmaf

Join Kali Hart's Reader Group on Facebook:
https://www.facebook.com/groups/1106383086217315/

Visit Kali Hart's Website:
https://www.kalihartauthor.com/

Made in the USA
Monee, IL
18 May 2024